FREEDOM

I hope you will relate when I say, my new life began with incarceration. I sat In the Columbus Ohio workhouse with twenty-one other woman.

I felt fear, despair and hopelessness in my heart while my face lied saying "I'm in control". I asked myself, "How did I get here? (Could it be the .001 gram of crack cocaine found on me?) No. "Could it be my inability to stop the using drugs? "No.

believe it was my call for help;"God please help me stop, I don't know how, or what to do". I believe the day the police took me out of my car because of drugs and took me to jail; help was starting to come. Being court ordered for treatment was the next level of help.

Now I had a choice to make...Get clean, stay clean or go back to the workhouse. "Why is that place called the workhouse? You might ask. You will not do a drop of work. It maybe my mind they required me to work. Two days was long enough.

My choice of treatment did work a long with 12 Step program and a sponser. Clean date 02-27-99, by the grace of God.

To the newcomers I can say, "I have never relapsed. I believe the more service work I do along with working the steps the better my chances are for staying clean.

Addiction

If The Drugs Don't Get

U

The Lifestyle Will

By

Roxanne C Fredd

Keeping it 1000

IN 2010

Second -Addition

Also Available from Roxanne C. Fredd:

Gas Card:

Coming soon

Detective Rodney MacAfee

Case of:

Gas Card & the Five Million Dollar Horse"

Additional copies maybe ordered directly from of Roxanne C. Fredd

P.O. BOX6448 Columbus, Ohio 43206

USA Telephone: 614-445-6131

Amazon

Book Store

Cover jacket design Book Layout: Roxanne C. Fredd

All Photos: Personal collection of Roxanne C. Fredd

Copyright ©2009, by Roxanne C. Fredd

ISBN: 978-0615-34600-7

First Print: Jan 2010

Library of Congress Cataloging-in-Publication Data

Dedication To

God first who is the head of my life.

My parents, Gibson W. Sr. and Rosa Lee Coleman

To my nephew Christopher Coleman known to the world as C. C

R.I.P

To all that gave me love, support and encouragement,.

Callie Coleman, Little Lisa Coleman, Yvonne Sayles and my best
and dearest friend Nicole Martin thank you for all your help.

Then to my teacher \tutor **CHAMSIL:**   Author, Poet Wontyme IV
Your Mynd Publications, good luck to you with your books

Locate him at: www.iamchamsil.com or

Email: chamsilthewriter@yahoo.com

Thanks to Joey Pinkney, for the "5 Minutes, 5 Questions series
(Check out my author interview at
http://www.joeypinkney.com/interviewed/roxanne-fredd.html)

To

All recovering addicted and or alcoholic people, coupled with
12-Step programs through out the world thank you. I believe
together you paved a road to fight off the disease of many
manifesting forms.

"I can do all things through Christ who strengthens me."

.Philippians 4:13

Table of Content

Part I

Part II

Part III

Roxanne Fredd is a throwback author. If The Drugs Don't Get You, The Lifestyle Will, takes the glamour out of the street life and shows you the nastiest, sweetest, most terrifying aspects. Fredd penned a fast-paced world of gritty dialogue and unflinching reality where dope fiends and dope dealers are on a parallel track to hell. Readers beware.

Joey Pinkney, Book Reviewer at JoeyPinkney.com

Preface

Based on my eleven years clean and sober, I share my personal interpretation of a deadly illness known as addiction. My degree on the disease of addiction came from knowledge acquired through pain and growth through life. While on my quest to enlighten how I rid myself of all drugs and alcohol, I visited correctional and treatment and talked to groups of men and women of all races and ages. The recurring themes of our conversations were, "Drugs and lifestyle, had been their downfall." I must say that it felt good being able to go into a prison then walk back out the same day. Not having to live with those slamming steel doors day after day for years of my life was a blessing. Every time I went inside a prison, I thanked God that this was not my story.

Then the sting of prison slapped me personally, with my husband and son going into prison. Drugs and Lifestyle had boldly taken over my home with and without my permission. I make that statement because I saw the power of the lifestyle consuming the two men in my life. I vividly recall the big guns, then even bigger guns, that were in what was supposed to be a secret place inside our home.

Question: What is a 'Lifestyle'? Well, this is my personal interpretation based on what I have witnessed in my fifty-six years of life. Lifestyle, "The way a person will act or portray him or her self to be in a day-to-day existence." Thus, there are many types of lifestyles. I feel safe to say that my eleven years clean and sober is a lifestyle for me. Except the lifestyle inside this book, talks of a force powered by destructive, self-centered ways of life. It has no respect for the well-being, property, or safety of others. A kill or be killed mentality between people on the street, also known as "the block." This type of lifestyle took out the men inside the pages of this book. That insatiable hunger for fast money, power, and the look of a baller was what they went after, not considering the price that they could ultimately pay for it.

My husband, Booker T, and I felt compelled to write this book of fiction, *"If the Drugs Don't Get You the Lifestyle Will"*! We spent several hours together on weekend visits at the federal prisons, talking about some of the dumb things that he went through and saw others do while out there on the streets, submerged in the lifestyle. Thus, we collaborated to create a heartfelt chilling story of sex, drugs and a lifestyle that has manifested itself into a book of recovery. For all that would like to know, my husband was and still is in recovery. Five years clean did not stop the prison doors from opening up to him and locking him away. Drugs are what he **sold**, and the lifestyle was what gave him the mindset to think it was perfectly fine to do so. Unfortunately, it was also the lifestyle that told him it was okay to carry the big .45 caliber on his person, which gave him a feeling of imaginary power, as if it were legal.

While writing this book, we also thought of the many people coming out of drug treatment or prison thinking,

"Now that I no longer use dope, I can sell it."

Ha, ha, that is a big—old—joke... A kid can't sell all the candy, nor can a monkey sell bananas. We also have prayed that this book will help the ones thinking of trying their first drug as a fun thing to do.

To those of you that may find the content of this book's words and actions to possess a certain degree of harshness, I warn you, that the **Disease of Addiction is harsh.** To those of you that have no clue as to the power of this disease, the best way for me to explain it would be for me to ask you to, think of it as a deadly illness. Addiction is as deadly as Lupus or Sugar (Diabetes), because if not treated correctly, the person will die. **Discrimination** is not a factor or disqualification for the two diseases that I just mentioned. Nor is it for the disease of addiction. Neither is there nor has there ever been a cure to this disease called Lupus, Sugar (**Diabetes**) or **Addiction.** No-pill, no shot, and no drink of a tonic will cure these illnesses.

[9]

Although there is no cure, a full life in recovery is achievable, one day at a time.

" Addiction will affect four areas of a life"

A great number of those that will read this book may question themselves,

"Am I affected by or infected with this disease called addiction?" I can tell you that no one can answer that question but self. Many of you may use something to get high or call it a way to relax yourselves. You think that you are ok, because you can stop and get your life straight, only to return to getting high. I have learned that people focus on the ability of stopping, but not looking for that ability to stay stopped. Only after awareness of total unmanageability or finding one's self trapped in a strong state of despair, will a prayer for a desire to stay stopped come forth. Please take a pen, paper, and count up the money that you had given away in one day. After that, do one week. Try adding it all up, if you can. Just imagine how much you gave away this year. Then add all the years you have been getting high. Damn! That is a lot of money given away to someone you don't even know, even if it was at the bar.

Mentally, it will consume your mind to the point of not thinking **of** nothing else but it. When I say it, I talk of whatever it is that calls you non-stop. Your mind will not leave your mind alone. While you lie in bed and pray for sleep, your mind will not leave your mind alone. While at work or in route to and from work, it will not leave your mind alone. As you see your life go downhill little by little, you may tell yourself: "Everything is cool. I got it all under control." However, you hold inside your hands a shut off notice for the lights and the gas. Fear of this takes over your emotions. This brings a sickness to your stomach, a flipping and turning as if you had to shit very badly. That feeling I have come to know as "Dis—ease, feelings of your spirit!"

Whenever the feelings of fear hit your gut, the Dis—ease, feelings of your spirit comes after. To counter that feeling you may think all will be ok if I can just get some more of it. Maybe even buy a lot and sell some of it. Only it did not sell fast, so you keep it all for yourself. Then it was all gone.

Emotionally, you cannot trust your feelings. "Why am I crying? Why do I feel so full of rage, damn! I feel fucked up inside, and I feel no one likes me. I can't go to my mom's house, sisters, or brothers. Shit, why did I have to rob their houses?" All the lies I have had to tell just to have it.

Physically, your body will go for days without sleep or food when you use it. There will be days you can't clean yourself, because you have to be on the move for it. Food was outdated until it and all the money was gone. Unprotected sex with nameless faces gave damage to the body that the eyes can't see. Your body has encountered guns, knives, baseball bats and size eleven or twelve Timberland boots that keep attacking you, for no reason, twice a week. Your body may have pain, but use it and you will feel better every time.

Spirituality, Behavior will change and it will have you do things that you did not do before. You will do robberies, shoplifting and stealing from family and loved ones, hoeing/prostitution. Now the word 'Hoe' is another word that does not discriminate. No matter white, black or brown, man, woman, gay or straight, fat or thin, it will have you hoe for more of it. Moreover, a man will sell himself to other men for some of it. Abandon your children for days, shit some will sell their children for it. The sale of food stamps and the car; we will call it a packaged deal. We may agree that in the beginning the use of it was fun for all of us, but later it became work to have it, leading us to jails, institutions' or death; many will still follow knowing the end.

To the Dope Dealers

The five men depicted inside the pages of *"If the Drugs Don't Get U the Lifestyle Will"* shows some of the upcoming, plausible dreadful ends available for you. No matter what way a person chooses to use dope it will turn out with that lost-loser conclusion! Thus drug dealers I say unto you, "You're sick too, O—yes, just as sick as the ones that ingest that shit into their bodies. No matter what side of the fence you are on, every waken thought will be "where to get more good dope," to use or sell whatever the case, the thought is the same. Where can I get some good dope? Then after it's acquired, the thought changes to "I don't want to use it all up." However, the continued use/sale of it, tells me that soon it will be all gone. It will run out! Many dope boys or fiends are left with sleepless nights thinking where to get some more good dope. Can you see the never-ending parade of getting and running out of the dope? Therefore, to all you major drug pushers those that like to look down on us drug users, ask yourself this question; "Were there times you could not buy yourself something to eat, because all the money you had, was dope-buying money?" Keep it real with your muthafuckin' self, because I already know. Just like the dope fiend that did not eat today, because all he had was dope money, you

[13]

also let the dope run you, control you, tell you when to eat, sleep and clean your ass. However, you will say, no, it was the money, and if you do say that, than ask your self, "What gave you the money"?

"YOU AINT NO DOPE DEALER! YOU'RE A DOPE FIEND, TOO"

You are heading to jails, institution, or death"!

"Here's what I think, and have concluded"

Keeping the focus on ones self, I now understand the fact that I have and always have had allergic reactions to **it**.

(What is **it?**)　It is whatever is causing unmanageability in my life?)

Note: Doctor Dude, in the ER just told me,

"You're sick and nearly died due to your allergic reactions to fruit. Please know that every-time you eat fruit, you will land in the hospital ER, near dead needing treatment to save your life. So don't eat fruit if you want to live a little longer."

Seven times within two months, they had had to rush me to the ER for the some illness (eating fruit.) The same doctor working in the ER asked me, "*What* part of allergic to fruit do you not get?" He then went into all this long discussion about the harm to my body I was causing. As he talked the addicted person inside of me imagined, "*the dark red cherries at the store, the yellow bananas and how to get back to that store or what store to go*

[15]

to. " Too bad this damn disease may possibly have me try every piece of fruit inside a different store as I'm in denial of why I kept landing back in the same place. "The ER" as I tell myself, "it will be different with a different store or type of **It**." We could say I am living in a state of denial. There must be an understanding that fruit is fruit and a drug is a drug. Whenever I have just one, I land back in the same hellhole. Eventually, I ask this question,

" Do I want to keep using and keep going through this shit?"

For sure on my first day of life, my mother did not hold me in her arms and say,

"Wow! look at the little crack head, aint she sweet?"

Nor did the doctor that pulled me out of her cunt hit me on the ass then say,

"It's a crack head! Yes! We got us a fine-looking dope fiend here. She even got a strong mouth good for sucking dick."

My mother was optimistic of me and I let her and myself down along with my loved ones that trusted in me when I told lies to get money.

If you are unsure, take an honest look at your past. The disease of addiction has and will progress. If the above words are not your story then the word progressive should tell you that it would be your story. Continued drug use destroys the body, mind and spirit.

I do know about the most important person being the newcomer and it's not my intent to run them off with this book. Holding eleven years clean from all dope and alcohol gives me the right or should I say, qualifies me to talk about the end of the road and some of the sickest behaviors that go with and with out, the use of drugs. The people that suffer from the disease of addiction had sick behaviors before they ever picked up the dope. Sick behaviors, or call them behaviors of sickness, was there before the dope ever got into their body. We all have did and thought some of the sickest shit, and I can say "Our" and "We" because I too removed the dope, but still suffer pain from continuing to act out in sick behaviors, things that have put me into pain and harms way. Even without the drugs, I suffer with an inability of constantly being responsible for my own ass, thinking, "*My life fuck-ups are someone else's fault!*"

The first part of my solution was to stop the use of <u>it</u>. Just stop the use of whatever has your life unmanageable. Alcohol is dope, too. Drink too much of it and fall down on the ground face first, bounce off the wall or someone's car.

Second: get with a 12 and 12 .The programs will work to help you learn how to stay stopped from the use of **it**. Then learn how to stop the daily sick behaviors, and "**Find a new way to live**." In the recovery world, I learned to call doing something new, something new. Think about it! Change, has to mean what? (Something new) If nothing changes, then nothing changes. The word **denial** was one of the most harmful words I used in this work {refusal to accept the real} parts of this sickness.

As we refuse to accept how fucked up life is and has been for us, the disease grows stronger. Near the end, many may believe. "*I got this, I can handle this, and I aint hurting nobody but me, so get the fuck out of my business.*" This type of thinking has lead to the ability to stay fucked up for a long time and I'm talking years. The basic thought for a dope fiend is to think only of self. However, the people that love and want to see the best for us go through pain seeing us go down hill until a bottom hits. {**Denial**} has kept a person sleeping in the park through the summertime until that late cold ass fall night hits and no one is there freezing but self. If you, the reader, are wondering, about what you can do to get on a better track. Start with thinking less of self and more of others.

Please don't let the actions of these men, insider the pages of this book stop you. Yes you, the newcomer or you the person that paid only half of a bill this month so you could have money left over to get high. Then we have the people that give their children money, as a means to get them out of your hair, while getting high nonstop. Please come into recovery, because there is hope and help for you. If once you read this book you start questioning yourself about your own life and the use of or that you may want to stop the use of drugs, please give yourself a break and try a 12-step program. If you have children, there are meetings that allow children. However, you must keep them with you at all times. That means when you move they move. "No person need die from addiction today, because you have children and can't make a meeting."

"If the Drugs Don't Get U, the Lifestyle Will."

Is a story about men claiming clean time in recovery while living dirty by selling drugs? What happed to these men is typical for the life they lived. Just remember one thing about them all, they went to prison CLEAN! I also would like to say to the readers that might have a love one locked up.

Shit, that maybe damn near everyone that will read this book. Prison doesn't have to be a bad thing; it is whatever you make of it.

Try asking yourself, just what you can do to better your life today! Mind you, a thought will come talking about tomorrow. Please reread the words! Do you ever think about bettering yourself? **Answers today**

Opening

"If the drugs don't get u the lifestyle will!" A tale involving five men, their lives intertwined with recovery from drugs while in a lifestyle of selling drugs! Add in a number of homicides and we have drama. My name is Tweet! Booker T is my husband. Separately we talk of life with dope, and murder. Tweet's words are that of a spectator/wife. No, fuck that! To keep it real, I am a murderess bitch, who enjoys listening in on other peoples shit... Booker T. has his own cold words for you... We have no intent to give more time in jail for secrets told by us. Therefore, we have omitted a number of things the prosecutor's office could use for a conviction. To conceal the identity of the men in this book, we have changed their names. Nevertheless, their actions will show through to their friends and family inside the city of Columbus, Ohio. Thus, from us to them, "Hold your head up men, the truth may set your spirit free."

We start with this fact! "Not one of the men in this story claim, to be a true native of Columbus, Ohio." Each one moved here in search of quietness of spirit. The knot of emotional pain, deep—down—inside the pit of their stomach sent them running from home. Real stuff, each dude came to the city of Columbus, looking for what was already inside of him; they just did not understand the thing that made them feel the way they felt. Nor did they know how to accept and grasp hold of the feelings that go with the responsibility, of becoming a real man. Having a need to change feelings, opened the door to the over use of drugs for these men. All of them are ex-dope fiends that lived a life of hell, fighting off a disease called addiction. We talk of a disease that empowered these men an ability to fuck over loved ones and strangers without regret or remorse. The call for one more high was the tough bitch that forced big strong men into and out of treatment for drugs a number of times. (Please understand, we expose this seriously ugly part of life for these men. Not to belittle them as men, but to let you the readers know, that no matter what actions or behaviors they exhibit while clean, going back to getting high will never, be acceptable to them again.)

One of the most harmful behaviors these dope fiends acquired while under the use of dope was their ability to build a dead end road. They may have used different types of drugs but they all suffered the same behaviors that go with the **disease of addiction**. At some point in time, a dope fiend's hunger for more dope ends in a hopeless state of agony. Known to the recovery world as, their end of the road. There, they have no more trusted family or friends to fuck over. The house, car, job, friend, family and self-respect were gone. Damn! There just aint no more, one more get high. A part of the brain did realize they have been living inside of an abandoned house not suitable for human existence. On the other hand, maybe it was some old abandoned car without windows. No matter, the fog of denial lifted long enough for the dope fiends to see where their uses of drugs on a daily none—stop—basis, had taken them. That reality gave heart-felt sadness that brought forth a shout out to the world, the words,

"I'm tired of this life!" Those words said a lot if we combined the heart felt anguish with hunger for food and water. It is pure insanity to have not eaten for a number of days. Then fuse all that with the **awareness** of the smell that rose from one of the funkiest asses in the world! Awareness, yes awareness is a good word for when reality hits that twisted brain to realize the smell vented from their ass. So dedicated to getting high there was no time, to clean themselves, for the past three weeks. Damn! All this shit hits the dope fiends hard. This permitted them to see and feel the beast they had become almost over night. The **honesty** of what's real, right here, right—now—melts, down through their heart on into the soul!

[23]

That deep pain weakened them and caused their body to slither from a seated position down onto their knees! Their pathetic bodies kneeled over, balled up almost to a fetal position without lying down! Tears drown their eyes and over pour onto their cheeks. Head set dropped low, chin touched to the chest, while the sensitivity of a little boy consumed and forced a call out for a mother that cannot hear her son cry for help. The tears ran for a time then a shout came-forth in a slobbered plea, *"God--God –please, take-me-now, or free me from this life of pain and suffering, please--God! I don't want to live like this no—more--please—please."*

The voice softened and lowered as the word *"please,"* continued to flow out of the soul through the mouth! This we call hitting rock bottom, and from here, they can only go up one day at a time. I hope you can see why they would never go back to using dope! One by one, they came into recovery declaring 24 hours clean. Sickened and tired of life on an animalistic level to have eaten from the near by fast food trashcans they felt truly beat down to the level of **surrender**. The things the **12-step program** offered sounded damn good compared to where they came from. Not everyone entered into recovery at the same time however; as each man arrived, he became accepted into the little pack where he felt the love he had not felt for sometime on the streets. Here they would be until one by one they faded away

Journal entry **1**

Hello to you, my new, best and dearest friend in this world Mr. Journal!! My name is Tweet, and I need you to listen to all my thoughts, words and secrets. Please keep within these pages everything I'm about to share for the next thirty days. It would be so nice if I had a person to talk to as most people do, sharing their inner most secrets. However, where I come from, if two people know your shit, it's no longer a secret. I must have someone to talk to, which is why I need you Mr. Journal. Hear me clearly when I say, I'm planning to kill a man!

This dog, received the highest respect as head of six, bad men, here in Columbus Ohio. Even though, I have never held back, my own views on the man that are, "he isn't shit." My confirmation came with three of the six men sucked into Federal Prison, while the other two went to the State Prison. They all went down one by one all but the marked man. Tell me this, Mr. Journal, "how in the fuck is this bastard still on the streets gettin money"? I have thought about this long and hard, he has to be a dirty informant, snitching to the police to save his own ass, and that is why I'm all alone today. I know there is a thing called luck, but there isn't that much fucking luck in the world.

Hell, If luck is going around for people like that, I need to get me some. Thus, I won't end up in jail, after I cut off the marked man's head. Mr. Journal, our job is to trail him, and note his every move, this dog's pattern is what will get him killed. I have moved into a house three doors down from his crib. Yeah, that's right; as I sit on my porch drinking my coffee everyday I can see the flow of people coming and going through his door. I just don't understand how the Feds saw everybody in the crew selling dope and not this dude. I know the shit he's up to would take him to prison, for sure if I just complain to the law, although I feel that prison is too good for his ass, da man just need to be dead! Shit, real men--don't talk to the Feds, and I am a real man's woman, about my stuff. There will be an open window, of opportunity for him to pay me for being all alone. I can still hear the Judge declare, NINE YEARS. That is how long I will be with out my boo, my husband, Booker T. and my son Turtle—he got three years thanks to this marked man. I want to kill—em, O-yeah I got to kill—em, he can enjoy his free ride now, but when I play that slow song! "Pay Day"! He gonna pay me in full.

The Nosey Chick

Tweet:

Get-n high day after day with out trickin was a J.O.B. for me. Always, did have a hoe or two around my house that kept money and crack on the move through my door. After my two kids had gone off to bed, my hotel was open. From nine P.M until seven A.M ten dollars to rent a twenty-minute room was the price I charged. I had considered myself a crack head Madam. I took care of the girls at my house. During the day, the kids went to school and every one got some sleep, if we could. However, there were those three and four day runs that the crack felt so damn good, nobody got sleep. Everybody danced to the song called *"give—me—more, more, and more."* When that song played the girls did what ever, they had to do, to bring in dope money. Sometimes we had to put our money together to get that next hit of crack. As head of the house, I always got my shit off the top. Having cable, food, and a place to clean their asses was what the girls loved most about my place. As a bonus, they had LiL kids to play with, that prevented the sadness of not having their own. Some nights after the crack high was gone, and the girls were out in the streets, I would have time to think. Think back to before the crack came into my life. Who was I then? I was a person who enjoyed a new bright red Buick that I drove off the show room floor with zero down. I had a six-bed room home, and a hell of a good retail business, all gone up in smoke. I lost five long years of my life chasing that crack demon. Some days I can

[27]

still hear my cousin's voice inside my head.

"Well cousin, Do u won't to light up da bomb, or da bomb tuda bomb?" never—telling—me, that one of these bomb ass joints got crack in it, and I'm about to smoke my life the fuck away. Real shit, I can no longer hold resentment against my cousin, because there had to be something already wrong with me to have been looking for an escape from the reality of life itself. {*My mother was dying from the big C! With the help of my three brothers we made the decision to keep her at home, we did the damn thing. Our mother did not suffer with mistreatment at the end of her life from poor nursing.*} Thinking back on it all now, I can say I feel good about taking care of my mom, and I pray my own kids will do the same for me   I held a warm smile on my face for a second thinking back more on the past. Stay focused said a demanding voice inside my mind. I snapped back to my--business--at hand.   I must be ready whenever I set sight on that short piece of shit. I had been tracking him non-stop for two days. I saw him leave the corner store with some other scumbag; I knew I had seen dude before! Then it hit me, Hell-yeah, that there was Johnny-boy another piece of shit from the recovering world. Damn, if only I had a sprayer, I could get them both while they conversing and walking over to the marked man's car. His latest vehicle at the time was a green Bentley with black leather interior. All I could do was feel that rage, as my eyes held them close.

He seated himself in his car, while Johnny boy stood outside the car talking. Then he stepped back, the car lights, beamed out onto the road before the Bentley pulled away from the curb. This marked man was dead, and he doesn't even know it. I followed him in my rental car and we turned onto State Ave. I stayed on the anus of this piece of shit-ass man; I got up close but not close enough to be recognized. I felt a charge rush through my blood as I hold back and park up the street whenever he pulled over. One time while seated in my car, I witnessed a pair of street walk-in hoes going at each other. They seamed to be unsure about whose corner it was. It started with a good shouting match then ended with blows. Just like Dumb-ass bitchies' fight-in over crumbs when together they could have a whole slice. The glimpse of that shit took my mind back even deeper to my old life.

A crack head gypsy, I lived and moved from place to place. I ran from the law, all over the city of Pittsburgh. After smoking a lot of crack, paranoia set in, fear of one-times, (police), take my kids away caused me to move consistently. Nevertheless, no matter where I lived there was always some bitch ready to hang with me and sell that pussy so we both could get high.
"Dusty, I can't see' how you jump in and out them cars like that girl, aint you scared sometime?" I questioned while melting some crumbs of crack on a glass shooter hope-n to get a nice hit! As I held in the smoke, Dusty said,
"Shit, at first I was scared as hell, but I've been doing this thing for some years now and it's all about the money."
All this harbored inside my mind, while I sat back, in a dark blue rental car. I

[29]

patiently, awaited my marked man, to come out of his crack trap. Identifying with the hoes and crack heads on the late night street did truly take a bitch back in time. Back, to a place when I myself had used crack. Back then, I lived to use and used to live! Get-en high was a way of life for me. I did many things to keep from selling my ass like the other women. Except years of participating in that dope-fiend—life style, give me the opportunity to do what I said I would never do. {Sell my pussy to get high}

A slow Monday had my shit all fucked up, having got started getting high right after the kids took off for school left me wanting more. The girls were gone hours at a time, leaving my ass bugging for that next hit. I tried calling around town to borrow ten or twenty dollars however; it was the end of the month and everyone was out of cash. I hung up the phone and sat back thinking hard on where to get the next hit before the kids come in from school. A knock came on the door; I sprung my ass off the love seat to look out the window with big wishes that the person out there held a good hit of crack for me.

A disgusted look formed on my face as I felt my eyes narrow down. To see Raynell, a very tall fat huffing puffin drug dealer standing there, didn't make my day. He always stopped at the crib on his way home from work. Big money rolled some days and some days only $5 or $10. The best thing about him was all money counted as good money in his pocket. Raynell also had a thing for me. Often he offered me, two fat-twenty-dollar things of crack with hopes I would give up that ass. I'd laugh at his game and put one of the other girls onto him. That way I got cash for the room and a hit off the girls dope. I should be honest, I did enjoy the fact that he wanted to fuck me the way I looked most days.

"Ain't no money here today"! I whispered out the window with that sickened sound in my voice. Raynell looked up at me as he asked,
"So, Tweet u gone open the door today?" even though I know he heard what the fuck I said.
"Hold on!" I harshly shouted as I stepped back out the window then down the steps to the door.
"So what's up with u girl? Are you straight?"
He questioned before the door fully opened.
"Dude I see u got jokes with you today, shit aint--nobody got no money up in here, if you did not hear me the first time."
 I hesitated for a second then I shared my thought,
"But I was hoping you would be nice and let me hold one until."
Using a nasty ass tone Raynell repeated my word
"Until!"
"Sorry Tweet! I just don't do credit, that way I won't have to fuck nobody up about my money."
While I held the door open for him to leave, I began to look sad again. Raynell placed his hand on the door above mine. He then respectfully said,
"I still got them 2 fat ones for some of that thing down there," many words came into my mind. *"Damn, I wanted a hit bad and two of his pieces would be like having a fifty piece."* I put my head down and softly said,

"Come on in dude and it better be quick!"

He stepped fully in past the door to allow me to close and lock it behind him. I stepped by him to lead the way up the steps on into my living room, on over to the gold colored love seat where I had previously been seated praying for a hit. Raynell behind me now positioned in front of my face undoing his blue jeans. He clearly had a grin on his face, and I knew his brain was shouting,

"I'm about to fuck Tweet, the bitch that can't be fucked!"

His reflection was true. All the men in the area that sold, or used dope talked about me, and my code. (I never fuck while getting high.) I had no problem telling a dude up front *"no u can't see my tits and no u can't blow smoke on my pussy! If we are getting high then we're getting high and that's it!"*

Damn, on that one day with 6'2, 269-pound Raynell the code was dead and I assumed Raynell got a nice size dick, being a large man. I held it in my fist and moved my hand up and down the shaft to get it good and hard. Then jokingly, I questioned,

"So when's the last time you seen this big thing?"

He came back at me very nasty with.

"Put it into your mouth, I swear it will grow even bigger."

I placed my hands on his thighs and pushed him back some as I said,

"I'm good on that one baby." As I stood, and then turn around, I jokingly whispered,

"You asked for pussy so come get it"

However, before I bent over the arm of the love seat, I declared

"U to big to lie on top of me boo"

[32]

Without a word he went up into that black fuzzy pussy, I made sure I put that ass high up into the air so he could dig deep. Then I started rotating my hips giving up all that pussy to him! Shit he couldn't help but grab me by the hips to hold on to this wild cat. Next, he was making low muffled sounds while I worked that ass. I even used the muscles inside to grab hold of his dick!

"Whoa *baby! Hold up shit slow down girl! I aint trying to come so quick*"

On his command, I slowed the hip rotation down to a near stop, however; inside of my head I was thinking,

"Please just cum fucker!"

My holding somewhat still, did allow him to get his hump style going as he tried to play all up inside some pussy. He just may have got that shit off, but I trained my pussy muscles to grab a men's dick tight. Every time he humped that big ass brown dick up in my pussy, I locked on. Shit it didn't take long for him to cum after I put my C game down on him. My B game comes with good ass head and pussy. The A game calls for some of that ass hole, with head and pussy and that shit aint for every man. Finally, the bizz was over, he stood still with weak legs re-doing his pants before he reached into his pockets and handed out two of his fattest twenties. Holding my crack in the same hand, I used to play with his dick I walked quickly to the steps and on down to the door. I could tell he was weak as hell the way he was moving all slow. I questioned him as he stepped down the steps, where I held open the door for him to leave.

"You ok dude or do you need to sit and chill for a minute?"

He used all his manliness to move on to the door where I stood holding the

[33]

door-open. I was quickly patting my left foot on the floor showing my impatience. Finally, he walked past me out of the door. I seen he carried this big ass grin on his fat face. I think it was the grin of pure pleasure. That day Raynell made a comment to me I will never forget, he was getting into his fine ass car, when he said

"Tweet baby, I wish we could bottle that pussy and sell it, man we would be rich."

I tossed out the words,

"We! What-fuck'n—we, Raynell?" As we laughed, I had a chance to think of a good-come-back, for him.

"Damn, Raynell, if it was like that, I think u owe me some more pieces!"

He looked back at me and we both laughed a good laugh before I closed the door to go get my high on. As the years passed by, I found the everyday use of drugs in my life had a downhill regression.

That day was my first and only time; I gave up my pussy for some crack. That day with Raynell left me fucked up inside my spirit. At the start of smoking Raynell crack things was cool. I had some dope but as I smoked, I began to think what I had done to get that shit. I was no better then the girls jumping in and out of cars all night and day. I began to feel bad but it did not stop me from smoking and when it was all gone, it did not stop me from wanting more. (Fuckin crack ain't no joke.)

At the end of crack head alley, the crib my two kids and I lived in looked like a true dump with big holes in the ceiling in more than one room. The water was off so the toilets don't work, and we could not clean the dishes. Pots, skillets and cups stacked all over the counter and stove with mold covering them. Dog shit sat through out the basement and yard giving an odor that would take months to have washed away. This definitely was the worst it had ever been for us, I was letting my kids down. I didn't want to ask for help from nobody. I told myself as I continued to-get-fucked-up everyday, all day *"I got into this shit! And I can get out on my own!"* All types of things crammed my head on those late nights after all the dope was gone, the ugliness of my life sat there before me. There was no denying it; I felt fucked up and in need of help. I awoke in the morning in a state of desperation strong enough to take me to my oldest daughter Sherry's house to live. Except; I still took no action other than to keep getting high on crack every day. As I did so a voice of deep guilt on the inside of my head said things to me like "Hey bitch, *you're the mother how you gonna ask your daughter for help? What will she think of you? She just may call you a crack head bitch!*" All those

[35]

words brought with them the feeling of shame and with the feelings of shame came many tears. I tried not to let my little ones see me cry but, I felt so fucked up knowing that me, two kids, plus the two dogs are about to be put out on the street for no payment of rent on this fucked up house.

Finally, I decided to take action and reach out for some help. I walked to the pay phone in spite of the shit talking inside of my brain and made a call of desperation. A call for help was a sob of words mixed and mumbled up, but Sherry heard and felt her mother as I said
"I can't do this no more please come get us now."
Before I knew it Sherry was there blowing the horn of her car. Two kids and the dogs came out the door first smiling; I came out last dragging with me three large green trash bags of clothing, happy we were being-saved. While living at Sherry's home, Hank, Sherry's husband told me how he struggled with crack and over came it himself. He told me that it wasn't—until, he became sick and tired of being sick and tired of messing up all his money on payday did he get help. He knew he had two kids plus a wife at home depending on him to make it but he could not stop getting high every week. I listened to his story and felt it was a hope shot for me that maybe I too can stop using dope. However, it was not that easy for me. After two months of not using crack, I went back to getting high everyday, all day. Then I heard from someone, that the dope boys gave crack out that looked like fifty pieces up in Columbus, Ohio for twenties.

All that was twelve years ago for me, since then I have moved to

Columbus Ohio, pushed up on nine years clean, and married a cold ass young pimp named Booker T. out of Baltimore Maryland. O-yes and our lives were great until my marked man, came into our world and fucked it all up!

Wherever Tweet goes there, she is

Question for the reader,

Where are-u today, and are-u-where u-had hoped to be?

On the other hand, knowingly you took yourself to this place in

your life... Think of everyplace you wish you where?

What is your plan to get yourself there?

Answer:

Da Set Up For Prison

We've opted the words, set up for prison freely, because when a man or women are breaking the law, they are knowingly setting themselves up to go off to prison. Their names are LiL Don, Kid, LiL J, Roy, Tiny and Booker T. Being a part of the recovery world they all heard the saying, {*if the drugs don't get you the lifestyle will*} O-yeah they heard it, and laughed hard at that cliché, thinking it won't happen to me. Dee's men grew a strong bond together as the years passed on and clean time from dope accumulated for each one of them. All of them were clean with some years when I got to recovery and I had three years when my husband Booker T arrived. He was what we in recovery call a newcomer or the baby with six months clean. The men took him in for training to learn how to do whatever you want in life with out the use of drugs or alcohol because alcohol is a drug, too. A magnificent friendship started through the world of recovery, however; it carried over to their hunger for some real big, big money. They truly enjoyed doing shit together from the sample of some good pussy to the hit up on a jewelry store or two.

They even did money swindles on companies and banks, along with other things I dare not to share. Please believe me when I say they always got money together just not as fast or as much money as selling dope will bring to the table. It was about to be on and popping so let us go to where it began!

[39]

To the

Pastor's wife Mollie Marshall

Thank you for the self-sacrificing work you have done at

Smyrna Missionary Baptist Church

Ramses Bar

The men enjoyed dinner at Ramses Bar often without their better halves. Two or three times a week, I received a call not to cook because my husband was having diner at Ramses Bar with the guys. I questioned him and his friends about Ramses Bar. What type of place was it? I found out it was a nice quiet spot on the West Side. Then it happened! I had to meet Booker T. there. Hence, I saw and overheard for myself the night the men made a collective decision to sell dope.

Ramses Bar, was a small red brick building surrounded by a gravel parking lot. It was near eight o'clock, when I stepped out of my car, the rocky ground gave me hell to walk-through in heels. As I walked, I saw all types of nice vehicles parked in the lot and it looked to be full. I also saw three young suspicious looking dudes talking near the front of the building. I passed by them and gave a soft "Hello," prompting a silence to fell in the air. That stillness told me they were stuck gocking at my smoothness. Thank God, I made it up to the red entrance doorway without tripping on a rock. I had a frozen desperate look on my face, as I stood just inside the doorway. I looked all-around up and down the dark brown bar counter. Shit, every damn seat in the place was empty. An ominous feeling began to flow up my spine with the two more steps I took. I looked even more through this place for my husband. I spotted the bartender, a larger De-bow dude, with his face glued to the TV.

The lights set super low, made the room dark as hell. A single string of red Christmas lights that went around the full wall length mirror did help show me the ugly ass paint job. Black or deep dark chocolate some real shit-tie colors, plus beer posters here and there. Wooden shelves sat In front of the mirror with all types of full bottles of alcohol. I just stood there thinking what a hole in the wall spot. Then the good aroma of soul food took my stomach to a notable emptiness. My toast and coffee was gone from this morning. As I continued to look around, I whispered to myself,

"Ok girl, what the fucks going on here. Can't see anybody cooking shit up in here! Nevertheless, I smell some good soul food! The lot was full of cars, but where the fuck is the people?"

With a persistent pursuit, to find my husband, I looked along the left side of the wall. I saw a couple pawing at each other inside one of the four red leather booth. No-Booker T. Then I step to the bar where the bartender asked,

"Can I help you miss?"

Before I could answer, I saw a doorway at the back end of the bar, another room with brighter lighting. I stepped back, headed for the brighter room as I answered,

"No thank you."

The closer to the light I got the better I felt. I could hear voices and the smell of food got stronger. At the doorway I saw their heads all seated at a round-table. Boldly, I walked toward them knowing I smell and look damn good as a real woman should. Now fully in the back area of Ramses, I'm able to see a number of round tables full of people. Clearly, this place sold more food then alcohol in the evening. My husband stood as I approached with everyone casting hellos to me. As he handed me the knot of money I swiftly asked,

"Can I eat with ya'll?"

"Yeah, have a seat!"

Came from every man's mouth, before my husband Booker could kiss and rush me away.

Kid searched for a chair for me and placed it near my husband chair at the table. The wall was full of additional tan wooden chairs hanging from hooks. The wall behind the order counter was full of menus. I looked at the six men seated there while I waited for someone to come and take my order. All the men dressed in a fresh white tee, some V cut neck some crew cut. All with name brand jeans and high top white Jordan shoes. Their ages vary from 25 to 50 but they were all dressed the same.

While seated around this table enjoying our food, a combo of greens, fried chicken and macaroni, Booker T. joked with Tiny.

"Man your plate look like it got more food on it then ours!"

Kid leaned forward as he whispered

"Y'all know Tiny's fuckin the new cook working here and I'm almost certain she up in here cooking now!"

In his defense Tiny whispered back,

"Dude, I got the same amount as everyone else and it aint none of your business who I'm fuckin, " Tiny was sexing the sweet round thing cooking in the back; she even took out time to come to the doorway to give him a smile and hello wave. As the men joked back and forth with Tiny this dude walked into the bar looking fresh as hell like a big-time-dope-boy. He stood over at the counter to order some food when LiL Don nodded for everyone to look. Everyone took time to look over their shoulder at dude from head to toe in his fresh gear. Hell, I looked too but I was looking at him with other thoughts, seeing his body with a fine cut.

Right off, Booker T. sized the person for a hit, thinking of the size of his pockets. While the other men seen the dude had on the latest white J's with blue trim dem $200.00 joints. His jeans were brand name hanging off his ass, showing that he was a true Nigga. The label on the back half covered by the long sleeve white T showed a Bow, everything on dude's body was designer. Blinging hard with diamonds on the neck and large faces watch. LiL J opened the conversation up on how dude looks like he was eating well with dope game money. LiL Don began talking about how his dope selling game was banging before he started being his own best customer.

"Shit don't any of u men know nothin about selling dope" exploded out from Tiny's mouth, at the men seated at the table. He felt able to joke in view of the fact that he himself was an alcoholic not a dope fiend.

Roy responded, *"Fuck you! Stupid piss head alcoholic"* as everyone began to laugh hard at the cherry drink Tiny dripped down the front of his white T. Then LiL J started to talk about dope again. Now my eyes and ears are bigger then my mouth. Shit, I knew better then to say one word while they were into their talk. LiL Don agreed on how great it must be for those able to get that fast money that way. Then he threw out the fact, which he had been thinking on selling some dope lately himself.

"I believe I can do it this time man, getting that money way more important then getting high for me."

Everyone nodded and added their comment of never going back to using dope. Shit, I had to raise an eyebrow to that stuff while holding my husbands hand up-under the table. Some of these dudes at the table had good jobs and didn't think it was a good idea to step out and take the chances that go along with selling dope. LiL Don had no job; he lived off

An SSI check and his wife's money from her job as a traveling caregiver. The dope game sounded good to him and he was ready to get it started. Kid, a good, good friend of LiL Dons said, *"I'm in"* than the youngest of the pack, Booker T. spoke with a deep tone, *"Count me in too; shit I know I'm ready to get that money. I will never get fucked up that way again."* With the three of six on one accord, they made a group investment that kicked it off.

Week's later fast dope money flowed to them. Their dope business started out with crack cocaine. However, in the recovery world, we have a saying, "one is too many, and one thousand will never be enough."

I think that saying applies here. Before long their stock consisted of crack, weeds, powder cocaine, heroin, ecstasy, Viagra, and pills housing codeine {Tylenol 3, Percocet, and ect.} Now these dudes begun to act, and look like Tony Montana, taking it to the limit. Tight floating rims were the first things bought along with big medallion chain that said a niggah had big money on his plate. They soon added a code {If it don't make dollars it don't make sense.} LiL Don had the ability to get a bigger better deal from his peeps in New York City or somewhere up in the hills of West Virginia. This made him top dog, the go to man for large dope buys. Although all these men had connections from their past dope using days, no one could get true dope at the price LiL Don could. Damn, the price keeps going higher and higher coming out of LiL Don's hands. Greed is a thing known to breakup many friendships in the dope game and it was underway here with all these men. If any of these's guys use another connection for his re-up LiL Don had a real big problem with not getting any money out of the deal. The code changes to {if LiL Don doesn't make more money than u do it don't make sense.}

Kid, Da First To Fall

Kid was not hard to look at by the women. His honey brown skin tone mixed with a short built of five foot three made his stockiness look sexy. With 8 years, clean time, he was the first of five dudes locked up. One of the places the men would meet everyday was outside a one story building on Livingston. A place known as "Only for Today Club" most days they never went inside unless the coffee was fresh. Inside the building at 12 noon, a meeting went on everyday, for those that still needed to learn how to stay clean. As for others not needing a meeting, they stood around out front of the building smoking cigarettes. While smoking they speculated on how long some of the new comers would stay clean. The newcomer girls looked like fresh meat dressed up in their come fuck me clothing. It may take them a little bit of time to UN-learn how to dress and act likes a hoe. Until they do the men bet on who will be first to hit that ass. I stood out there to smoke and listen to other people talk.

"How ya'll like this shit here!
Was what LiL Don said while he closed the door to his latest toy at that time? {A tan color Lincoln Continental} It aint nothing for LiL Don to buy a new car every six months or take an old school car and re-do it over to his own liking. I'm looking at it but I don't say anything.
Tiny and Kid are in a deep conversation and do not respond to him either.

"Tell me niggah! How in the hell u gone leave some bitch's under-wear in my car? Fuck! Good thing I came out the house, before my wife did and saw that shit."

"My bad man, we looked all over for them things, and we couldn't find them! Where were they? Tiny questioned, with a smile on his face.

"Fuck you, Tiny you won't get my shits no more, so don't ask." Kid had a wife and five small children to feed.

"So how ya'll like my shit? Or you dumb muthafuckers can't hear today"

Shouted LiL Don when his foot hit the sidewalk

"I bet not one of you fuckas can guess how much I paid"

No one said a word, as the three men walked around the tan color Lincoln Continental checking it out.

"Two stacks, Bitches, that's all I paid for that one"

Both Kid and Tiny complimented him on a good buy.

"Well, you gone take us for a ride in it niggah?" questioned Tiny. *"Get in"*

The three of them got into the car, and went for a ride up on Cleveland Avenue looking at hoes walking the street. They like to point out the ones they already had suck their dicks and joke as to how good or bad the head-job was. One-sixty-one off ramp, to the strip club was the final destination. How do I know what they do? My husband told me that they always do the same thing after the meeting. Before long, the whole gang was there slapping ass, getting lap dances and shooting pool. Kid knew he had to go to work in the morning but stayed out late anyway. His philosophy in life was *"play hard to die happy."* Nice thought for a man that has no family to feed, but he had a

[48]

wife and two children.

His job as a supervisor of a furniture Company was a good one. His wife worked part time to insure being home, to receive the children after school. She drove a Town and Country Chrysler that had no payments, while Kid owned a suburban plus a Road Master payment free. The Road Master was the gang car; they all had to have a Road Master in the color of their taste. He did dream of more money and the selling of dope was a way of getting some of the things he had to put on hold. Often he had to tell himself,

"Not this pay but one day soon." It was tuff on Kid to be responsible and take care of home. As time went on Kid tried his best to get up everyday and go to work, after hanging out at the strip club, along with his part in the sale of the dope. His inability to go-to work after the late hangouts paid off. The layoff notice read; *"we can't use you any longer."* Kid could-not show the pain or fear that he felt going on inside his spirit that day he got fired. The old saying, *"Never let them see you sweat"* stayed on his mind all day as he interacted with other people. He went over to meet with LiL Don. As he traveled, he kept telling himself,

"Fuck that, I'll get another job, somewhere."

It appears Kid had forgotten the work it took to get this one job, some three years ago. See, when a niggah got five Correctional Institution numbers, behind his name, it aint so easy to get a good paying job like the one he lost. Time off from work went from day into week then into months. Kid developed a comfort in the words,

"I can't find a job." True shit, he doesn't want one. See a niggah can get very

[49]

comfortable out all day and night with the guys. Quickly denial of reality set in so good that he believed his own lies to wife.

He had to tell her something about why he aint never at home no more! His number one Lie,

"I'm out all the time getting money for us to live on, now that I aint got no job" It worked when she got on his back. Then when it did not work he used,

"I'm doing what I got to do for us to get by, baby!" Damn, all that was bullshit and she went for it.

In Columbus, we had a project called Greenbrier over in the South East end of the city. The gang used it like the Carter and took it all the way over. They moved from one crack house to another to elude the police. People went to jail when the police raided and some loss their rights for project housing, but none of the gang went down. The cops began to hit hard so hard that a get out of jail funds were collected. Call it Attorney or bonds man for Kid. For real, they all worked for LiL Don so who held all the get out of jail cash. Maybe LiL Don! Now I wonder who really came up with that plan, Let—me—think, was—it, LiL Don?

Kid lived in Greenbrier and his wife and children hadn't saw him in months maybe even a year. A phone call was all they received along with the money he would send through one of his boy.

He felt happy in the dope game, and loved the power that went with it. Crack heads around him twenty-four-seven, treating him like a god, running for crumbs. Boosters took Kids lists of clothing needs to the store, boxers, white T's and J-Box socks, for which he paid them in crack. His shit could cost three bills at the store but Kid paid only six of them things. Kid, also had a badass yellow bitch to lie beside every night. At first, it was just to feed his dick late night and then he fell in love. However, she was a cokehead, putting powder up her nose as fast as he got his new shit in. She got hers off the top {powder} before he could cook and rock it up. His money never was right, and LiL Don already got the word on the bitch and her big nose. LiL Don went to see Kid up in Greenbrier. When he entered the apartment door, Kid had a seat on the couch with the yellow chicks head lying on his lap. There were four other people there chillin that quickly, got up and left after they noticed the 45 gun on Lil Don's hip. LiL Don stood by the couch and looked down on the girl wondering why she never moved to leave the room. Then rudely LiL Don asked, Kid,

"Do you want to tell the bitch to get the fuck out or should I tell her?"

Kid responded,

"I got this" as he softly pushed at her arm then said, *"Baby, us men got business take a walk for me, please."* Without a word, she got up and left the apartment. LiL Don then set down on the other end of the couch and questioned,

"Kid man, I need to know what the fuck's up with you and the money, man. The money keeps coming up shorter and shorter. Are you smoking this shit

[51]

niggah! Did you relapse, or something?"

Kid just shook his guilt-filled head while looking down onto the floor. He tried to speak out with an answer, but his throat was full with shame. Then a deep muffled sound broke through.

"My girl got a habit and it costly for me."

"No *niggah! This shit costly for me"!* Shouted LiL Don, then he ordered, *"Man drop the bitch, she got to go,"*

Kid looked sick and never did confess nor protest his love for her. He just replied, *"Ok man, she gone."*

He never did let her go, so the money continued to be fucked up.

After weeks of more shot money, an aggravated LiL Don called on Booker T. who was up in the short north end of town doing his thing. The caller ID read LiL Don

"Hello "

"Booker, man I need you to go and check on Kid, see if he still got that bitch hanging round his neck for me."

"When *you need me to do that shit?"*

"Now niggah! If it was later, I would have called later."

"Ok, Ok, I'm on it, I'll call you back"

Off he goes to Greenbrier to check up on Kid and this bitch. It was half past five when Booker T. rode around for one or two seconds before parking on the backside of the jets. Kid was not outside.

He stopped through some of the traps he sat in with Kid in the past, but he wasn't there. *"Now where the fuck this nigga at,"* blurted Booker T. while he walked. It was not until he rounded one of the complex buildings at the back end did he see a crowd of fiends on the front walkway steps.

"Hey, anybody know where Kid at"?

A yellow tone bitch steps out and volunteers to show him where Kid was. She led him to a nearby building and on into the hall and up the steps. Her ass was looking good from where Booker T. was, so he smacked her on that big juicy ass. She laughed and everything was cool, until she got in front of Kid. Now this bitch made a big thing out of him hitting her ass. (**Pussy**) Yes, pussy is one thing other than money, that will and has taken two friends to blows. These two came near to throwing blows as Kid's voice was high tone when he ordered Booker T.

"Keep your hands, off my shit dude, or we gonna do things, and that's real Book."

Booker T.'s last word while he walked out the door and down the steps where loud and clear.

"Man, fuck you and that yellow bitch--fuck'n cokehead, she aint your wife, you need to be gettin your ass home to check on her. Fuck that bitch right there and fuck you too."

Booker T. knew he was wrong to have done what he did but it aint like five foot three inch, *175 pound Kid* can throw down with six foot two inch, 195 pound Booker T. shit the man had to be just doing a show off for the bitch. Once back inside his car the call went out to LiL Don

"Man that dude is gone; he must have lost his damn mind to go up against me, over that bitch."

"What *Happened?"*

"I hit the bitch on the ass, the muthafucka asked for it as she was walking in front of me up the steps."

"You telling me, she asked you, to hit her on the ass." Lil Don questioned.

"Fuck no man, her ass asked for it, looking all good in them pussy cutter shorts"

"Book, man, I--tell—you, all the time, u sick dude"

LiL Don continued to place alleged insanity while the two men laughed hard about the bullshit. Later about three in the morning, Booker T. came into the house still upset about that shit. He woke me for his eggs and ham as I cooked he talked to me.

"Tweet baby, listen to this shit man, I'm still hot as hell at Kid from earlier today. Look I was up north doing what I do, when Lil Don calls me to go check in on Kid's. He been fuckin around with a yellow bitch that wont stop snorting up the shit, and Kid was supposed to been done drop the chick. So why Kid gone call me out to fight over her?"

I was lost on the whole story so I asked,

"What you mean fight over her baby?"

With a dummy look on his face, Booker T. tells me,

"Ok, I hit the bitch on her ass, when we were walking up the steps to Kids crib,"

My reply without changing my facial look was.

[54]

"Now-really and you don't understand him being upset with you?"

Booker.T truly showed how upset he was by shouting,

"Right she aint his wife. She just a bitch and all Bitchies are fair game to us."

With that statement, I had to walk away from him although I spoke loud while I did so when I said,

"Well honey, she must not be on that available list yet." With that answer given to him, I went back to bed.

Trust, often an overrated issue, left LiL Don bugging all the time. He had pushed everyone away but Kid, as the only individual still working for him in the Greenbrier area. Kid didn't stir outside the Greenbrier area for a little over a year. His re-ups, delivered to him; someone trustworthy collected the money for LiL Don.

It was a Friday morning with a strong cool breeze that LiL Don called Kid and told him; he wanted him to be over his crib today for a talk. Tiny picked up and dropped Kid off about 3PM. The two men chilled and talked until 5PM, Then Booker T. showed up.

Ok, time for Kid to go back to Greenbrier, and that was when it turned all fucked up for Kid. LiL Don tells Kid to take a toss car and drive himself back to Greenbrier along with the dope he just got from him. Everyone jumps into a car, three cars, pulling out from in front of LiL Dons crib.

LiL Don in the lead driving his own car pulling out from the curb, Kid drove behind him in the toss car while Booker T. drove his own car, bringing up the rear. All three cars on the move until the red stop light on Main and Kimble. When the cars pulled off again the officer known as Batman, come out of no-where. He pulled up long side Kid's car, not behind it because Booker T. was there, but right beside Kid's car. They pointed at him to pull it over. The red, white and blue light was on and Kid worked his way over to the curb. Booker T. slowly, said *"What the fuck!"* As he drove on by, slowed down some, tried to see what was up with this bullshit. LiL Don kept it straight back to his crib. By the time, Booker T. got down the road a good ways; he had me on the phone. *"Tweet it looks like the police got Kid."*

"Baby, where the fuck, are you at and what the hell is going on?"

"I'm by Rhoades Street, near the drive-through where I can get turned around to go back up Main."

There was a pause then he described to me what he was seeing. Kid seated inside the cop car gettin a 50 run on him; two more police cars that pulled up and Batman was looking through the seats of the car for something. As Booker slowly passed, he heard the one police known by the name Batman, shouted,

"I got it, found it"!

Booker did not hear the rest because he had to keep it pushing on pass but he knows deep down inside his spirit that Kid was gone for sure. Booker T then said, "Hold on baby, I have to call Lil Don,"

So I held while he dialed LiL Don's Phone, as it wrong he switched back opening up to a three way. When LiL Don answered, Booker T said,

"Cops *got him man, thay got Kid man, and you need to get some of that, put away money together to get him out"* With a nasty tone Lil Don came back with,

"What put away money, Kid haven't got none of that shit, his bitch sniffed part of it up and his wife and kids got the rest. Shit, I will see what I can do, Okay, ha Book, I'm doing some shit now, talk at you later man." click.

Kid was gone, he has to do a State bit, touch down the end of 2009. His wife the one he kicked to the side tried to stand by the father of her children. Took them to see their dad, she also put money on his books when she could. For that, I say she stuck by him when she could have said, "Kick rocks dude"! Then I heard some people talking as I often have over heard shit about people. The word was that LiL Don had the niggah in the beginning, for the first six months with a little money. Then I heard that Kid's wife went to Lil Don for help on money for her bills and her husband's books .This was with-in Kid's first year down, the nigga had her up in the hotel working for that money. I'm talking about the bitch had to do something strange to get that change. Then top it all off with him not making one visit to see his main man. I have said," Lil Don Aint shit" and I will keep on saying it!

To listen to Lil Don talking about his love for Kid around other dudes that don't know the real stuff that went down, it would sound like he was a part of the mans bit but he aint.

OK, now ask me the question, of how I know Lil Don Aint doing jack shit for the man. Okay, its like this, I had a friend that went down and housed with Kid in prison, this friend sent me a letter that told of how bad things were for Kid on the inside. He had a hard time without money on his books. On some real shit, my friend's letter read, kid has no food or toiletries. Then he asked, could, I ask LiL Don to send some help to Kid please.

[58]

Next to fall

I think of Roy as a nice guy. To me he was something like a momma's boy, too bad he got married to an ungrateful bitch. I say that due to my listening in, or call it overheard, when he said, *"She is an ungrateful bitch!"*
"She always asked for more, but not willing to put in the work to have more." That was what Roy informed Tiny of in front of me and some other people in front of the club on that day. I myself have not associated with her nor do I desire to. Roy also had a set of twin baby girls age 5 and one son age 11. His day job was as an Officer of the Courts at the Columbus Court House. Roy's clean time from drug use was 7 years. On the weekend, he played the bass guitar for a jazz club. On Sundays, he played for the Church. Often he and LiL Don, a want to be drummer, would get together and have a jam session with other dudes with instruments from the recovery world. Roy was damn good; I pray someday he will make it to the top.
Roy had a job and his friend's sold dope, no-way could he not see the bling, bling on his friends. As they get fast money from selling dope, Roy looked on. He wanted what he saw but felt confused; he questioned self and others near to him if he should try it. His thinking was he needed a plan to get into the dope-selling thing. Often he hung out with my husband and the other men on late night runs. Roy's problem was he did not really know how to start out his business. How could he approach a person to make a dope sale?

[59]

Roy and I ran into each other at the gas station on Parsons. As our gas pumped, we talked about the dope game.

"Tweet, please tell me what you think about me getting into the crack game?"

I looked at this six-foot 205-pound dark chocolate overgrown baby and tried to keep it one, thousand with him when I said,

"Roy, *those crack game aint for everybody! Shit, it takes a hard heart to not feel bad when you sell that stuff to people we have come to call dope fiends. Answer this question after you think on it, "Will you be able to take money off a chick that you know got babies at home to feed or tell her no when she ask to suck your dick for one more hit?" Dude' the type of things that go on in that world aint for you Roy, but we all need our own experience so do what you feel you got to do for you.*

Later that day when I talked to my husband I told him of that conversation. It was about a week later when Booker T told me, *"Roy workin for Lil Don. He went to LiL Don to learn how to become a hustler. That short shit puts Roy to work for him. If there was, a sale going on, Roy gets a call ordering him to run, jump, and shit just the way LiL Don said do it."*

"Roy, I need you man, can u get here to my crib, quick man?"

"Yap, on my way"

"Roy, I'm talking right now man, if you can't do it say so!"

"Look man, I'm on my way!"

Some people can multitask but Roy could not, his stuff was one track and because of that, LiL Don was able to use and take advantage of him, just plain use him the fuck up. Roy did build up his own customers. Nevertheless, when the order calls came he had to go see Lil Don to make the sale. Lil Don gives him just what he needed to serve that one dope run. Booker T. told me he was going to question Lil Don on that shit. He did tell Lil Don that aint right and asked him.

"Why u working that man like that?"

Lil Don came back with, *"Niggah! Just work your shit, and let me work mines, I pay him for what he does."*

Booker T. told me how he bust out laughing hard in Lil Don's face at that shit then said,

"Get the fuck out of here niggah! U don't pay that man nowhere near what he would be getting out there on his own"

Next, I over heard Booker T. on the phone talking with Tiny that he took Roy with him up in the Hampton Court Apartments. He showed Roy how the biz really goes. They hung together all day until late night. Booker T. told Tiny, he felt bad about that last stop. Booker T. called his boy to see what's up at dude's dope spot.

"Ha my nigga Booker T. what's good?"

"Not much what's up with you?"

"Man, I'm about to get my dog some head come see."

"When you doing this?"

"Now motherfuckah, but if you comin I can wait, but not long."

"Cool I'm on my way."

Booker T never said where or what was going down. When they entered the spot, a number of dudes stood around in a circle, shouting damn! Roy and

Booker T. worked there way through, up front to see what was jumping off. A gold and brown pit bull dog over a young girls face hump--ping like crazy. The girl lay on her back on the floor up on pillows sucking the dog's dick. Roy stood and looked for a time it was as if his brain and eyes could not understand what the fuck was going on. Then it all came together, she and the dog where having sex. Roy stepped back away from the floorshow, he felt sick then sicker. His stomach was flipping near vomiting level as he walked from the house. Booker T. stayed and questioned dude why he did not wait for him before starting the show. Dudes answer, "The bitch man, the bitch wanted to get a hit of crack before she put in the work. However, she can't get shit until my dog climax and I see the juice in her mouth."

On the ride home, Roy sat back quiet for a long time then he said,
"That shit there was not right! I call it fucked up, to take advantage of the sickness in someone else like that!" Booker T. had no words for him other than a, *"Good night"* when he dropped him off at home. LiL Don heard about the two-man hangout and got real upset about that one. Now he's acting weird toward Roy thinking he may go off and do his own thing with out him as a boss. The gang seems to be growing apart fast; the ones that see LiL Don's real color have started to pull away from him. While among themselves, they say,
"LiL Don Don't fly straight no more." After a half, year of jumping for little or nothing Roy never got a package of his own.
Some may say he got the best way out from under the gang, with blessed not

to go to jail. However, he lost his clean time. Yep, he got high, the ultimate no, just say no in the world of recovery. In recovery, we do find those that use drugs and alcohol. They come get hugs and receive the suggestion too "Just keep coming back."

How bout the drug pushers, pimps, molesters, killers, thieves, con-men/women we got all that too, but we just don't use no dope, and most feel damn good at the end of the day about themselves because of being clean. There was no way of knowing when Roy, will get back to not using again. Once that demon got out to do harm on the world it won't be easy to put it back into the cage. One is too many and a five thousand never enough. The doors now let open for Roy to lose his job, family, friends and life. So was he lucky or was he lucky? There's another question just as hard to answer, "Is the glass half-full or half empty?"

We thank you for joining us in marriage

Pastor

Bishop Fred L. Marshall of the Smyrna

*Missionary Baptist Churc*h

Journal Entry **2**

Ok, Mr. Journal, it's been two weeks now, what have we seen the marked man do? One: He never comes out of the house until after five PM. In addition, he never goes into the house before five AM. He's alone most of the time, riding in his car, with the music banging louder then hell. This could be a good thing for me, if I go for him in the late night. I must decide how I will kill him. You know one thing, Mr. Journal, I think I would have been a good hit woman, for the right price. I heard it stated somewhere, "Killing the first one is the hardest thing for a person to do." Shit, I did that one kill already, so this one here gonna—be-a-piece-of-cake. I must be honest with you Mr. Journal, sitting in this car all alone, for long periods, is hard on my mind. I get to thinking about Booker T. and his Bitchies. Aint no way I could ever have told him how hurt I was. Him out there all the time, fuckin this girl and that girl. Shit, he did try to tell me, he aint fucking them chicks, and that a pimp don't have to fuck his hoes to put them out to work. Right! I know he tested the product, to see if it was sellable. Fuck that, all I'm feeling now is when he comes home from prison, there has to be some different shit going on in our lives, if we're to stay together.

Wherever she goes there, she is

School Them Bitchies

Chickies always ask-n me, *"How u get the finest looking man on the block."*

"How come he jumps for u when u ask for something?" I try to school bitchies how the game works, but they too hooked on stupid to see the real deal. It took a man to teach me how to think for my man, live for my man, and if need be, die for my man. If a woman keeps her pussy right, her crib right, and her head right, her man will not go nowhere. Every man got a little boy inside of him, and every man got' a dog inside him, too. My job as his woman will be to provide his every need as far as cooking his food the way he likes it, bathe and pamper him when he comes in super tired. I also use a soft voice along with a soft touch to make him glad to be home at the end of one of his most fucked up days. Clean all his clothes, paying special care to keep his white T's white. Have them pressed for him to change into through out the day. Never question him as to when he will return home, because that can turn into a lie. Last two things are, if you plan to keep your man, go to bed dressed like a freaky ass chick and be prepared to ban with all his hoes if he ever goes to jail. If or when you get that call, "I'm locked up!" Be smart enough to keep money on his books and take him some fresh white underclothes. Be strong

enough not to fuck his so-called friends. Niggah's will try you, just to have the ability to say, *"She aint shit, because I fucked her nasty ass."*

Real bitches do these things if her man goes down. As Booker T's wife, I'm aware of just about everything that has gone on in my husband's game. His money, his bitches and his Nigga's he hang with, on a need to know basis. Whenever my man comes home, we talk about everybody and everything. This puts a stop to someone shocking me about some shit. There's very little Booker T. could do that would shock me, because I know what he's capable of. (You the reader fill in the blank) I don't have to, because I damn--well know him just as he knows me.

Tweet in love

We met on a cool Saturday night in June; I stood at the pool table in the recovery club, I had three balls left to win the game. Booker T. stepped up from behind me put his right arm around my shoulder pulled me close to him, then whispered in my ear with a deep, deep voice "Hello Tweet, guess who?" I had no clue of who it was but the sound of his voice opened up my curiosity. After he stepped out in front, I knew I did not know him but I planned to. See I had two men at home and I was tired of them both. We all slept in one queen size bed and most every night there was some fuck'n or suck-in going on in that bed. They both worked at the same job calling each other brother. Being the chick I am it takes a hell of man to handle me. Booker T. being twenty-five thought he was the man to do it, and if he didn't, well at least he tried.

In addition, I didn't know it but he had questioned other men around the recovery club about me. (Who is that chick Tweet?) They strongly suggested he stay away. Joking with him that he was too young to handle a chick like me. That only raised the lust within him. So he took my number and called me that night, his words where spellbinding to me, as my pussy got wet with anticipation after each time we talked. The next Saturday night we chilled at his place. That night I felt some shit with young Booker T. that took two men to give me. His sex-game came right, and the way he ate my pussy, licking my clit on the left side, just the way I like it. Most times, I had to school a niggah on what to do, but not Booker T. Then when he felt the time was right, he came with that big fat, long ass dick. Damn it was more then I could handle but I dare not say that aloud to him. My mind and my pussy were shouting" Hell no." My pussy walls felt a mixture of joy and pain. It was then I started think-in of that movie Damien how she went to bed with a man that packed more then she planned. Shit, didn't he flip that bitch over, and start diggin up into her ass? Fuck, what have I gotten into? Shot in and out of my mind along with the good dick going in and out of my pussy. I asked myself again,

"What the fuck have I got myself into this time"?

He felt it around his dick that I'm not built for all he had to give, so he took it easy on me, while we continued fucking on into the early morning. It was not rocket science to know I needed to drop the two zeros and keep the young hero. That morning after we got out of bed I went to the bathroom and then stepped into his kitchen. My plan was to cook up some bacon and soft scrabbled cheese eggs. Booker T. came out the bedroom with a towel rapped around his waist looking sexy as hell when my cell phone went off for the um-tenth time since last night. He looked at me and we knew it had to be one of my zeros wanting to know my where about. Booker T. nodded his approval for me to answer the call so I did. With one hand I held it, flipped it and said,

"Hello"

The voice was loud and deep *"Where r u Tweet?"*

Quick answer I said,

"I'm at a friend's house."

[70]

"All night right, all fuckin night, Okay what's his name?

The line went silent with him waiting for his answer and me not saying shit.

He tried again to get the truth out of me when he said,

'I know u aint with a girl so what's his name?"

Now I learned a long time ago to go dumb when you don't know what to say and answer a question with a question. Therefore, I asked,

"Why?" "Why are you asking me that?"

Again with the *"Just tell me the name?"*

Booker T. had overheard the demands placed upon me so he said loudly,

"Tell him; tell um, my fuck'n name." Loudly, boldly, Booker T. spoke.

"Tell um my name" letting the man know for sure I was out with some other man all night.

"His name is, Booker T"

I uttered softly while awaiting an explosion to come back at me. The curse words did come at me but I did not hear them.

It was at that time I realized {I didn't know this man's whole name} damn I done sucked his dick and fucked him all night and I don't even know his whole name. Damn, just stamp, tramp on my forehead.

Sacrifices are necessary whenever we change levels of life. Now a younger man with no job had me mesmerized, no longer am I the boss controlling the show. Booker T. had now in charge, and was nice enough to give the two men one week to move their things out of their house. Until then I stayed with him at his place. The day after he fucked me I gave him keys to my car, a copy of my debit card with the pin number for a bank holding two hundred plus and a key to my house. All I desired was more of Booker T. and he was there for me. Although ever bitch that laid eyes on him desired him too. When you got a niggah like this, look out cause at anytime a bitch could be smiling in your face while ready to snatch your ass out the co-captain seat. To counter something like that I quickly became his all-in-all, doing all I could for him. First, I sucked him out of his sleep every morning; he loved that shit, because he never had a chick do it as I put it on him. Then I cooked his food to his liking ever day or night. Fuck how I feel; my man has to have a home cooked meal. Conclusion: cleaning and not complaining about small things made me the bomb. Next, we started talking about marriage. Ok, cool that will be nice, but I'm 42 and you're 25 what do you see in me? Ok no answer! Next level I'm buying TVs', trucks and 100-dollar hats. Yes, I'm going in to debt but he's worth it. Booker T. went to work driving for a Temporary Agency. Income Tax checks he purchased my dream car, (convertible), along with clothes; baby has to look good. To top that off, he got down on one knee at the 12 noon meeting and put a ring on my finger for all the bitchies to see who the fuck he's in love with. OKay, I have to take it to a level he cannot match. After deliberating long and hard, it hit me "Three some." Since we lived in the hood and I had no call girl numbers I hit the track one night and picked up the finest girl on the block.

I told her, *"I need you to join me in suckin my man out of his sleep, then we will all do whatever he says, your job will be done whenever he cums. I got thirty-five dollars. Will that be Ok for you?"*

"Works for me but I would like to be paid up front." I laughed at that statement as I thought to myself *do I look stupid to her.*

"No baby, here take half now and more when you're done.

The two of us tiptoed into my bedroom where Booker T. lie

asleep, I nod and point to this sweet sexy thing to get undressed as I did the same, then we got started on the job of sucking him out of his sleep. At first he just made noises of pleasure! However, no two chicks suck dick the same way and he knew right off it was not only me down under the covers. With one quick snatch of the covers, he saw his gift for the night. With a puzzled look from him our eyes met and locked showing I love you without the utter of a word. I then spoke up and said, "You're the boss daddy give us your command!" His first order was for me to lie back on the end of the bed so she could eat my pussy while he slow fucked her from behind. Our eyes stayed on each other whispering, "I love you's" repeatedly. The girl ate me up on a good climax when he seen I couldn't take no more. As I push back away from her, he stopped fucking and let me up. Step 2, just he and the chick are in the bed and I set to

the side.

[73]

Damn, I had seen what a man with his size dick can do to a girl on the porn movies, but to see it live and in color, it looks like he don't care about the pain he put on her. As I watched him dog, her pussy out I had some thoughts come to mind. One was *Damn I'm glad it aint me,* as she screamed and screamed, my next thought was

May-be I should pay her more money for all that,

"Not," Thirty-five dollars it will be.

Yeah, that's real fucked up, how that young buck doing her pussy, but that's the girls JOB so take that dick. When it was over, I returned the hoe to her corner. Booker T. was standing in the shower when I got back to the house I walked into the bathroom and sat on the toilet seat. The shower curtain are clear plastic and allowed me to look at him as the water ran over his six foot one, pure chocolaty perfectly shaped body. "Just look at that six-pack", I whispered to myself then he turned and damn that Y cut on his back had me ready to fuck, but I knew he's tired so I just sat still. While doing so I said to myself

"Now top that Mr. Booker T." then I said to him

"So tell me? Who's the coldest bitch you ever loved?"

He had to say, *"You Tweet my wife to be"* O-yeah, that's right, that's right I'm bad, who's bad. The song I was singing to myself when he ordered his cheese-eggs with toast. Happily I went off to the kitchen still singing my song *"Who's bad.*

Not long after that, things took a turn and I became introduced to the pimp inside of my man.

[74]

These days I hardly see him, he's out on the grind getting that money day and night. This all started some years ago. I have one request of him, get here before the birds start to sing, don't let the sun beat you home, so far he has kept up with my demand unless he's in jail. This was how life went for me being married to this fine ass man.

Does that shit hurt? Yes, it's painful but I have to act tuff as if I can handle it. I had to keep the code of {never let them see you sweat}. On those long days and late nights when he's out, hell yes I sweat sitting home by myself. I don't think a bitch can take my man, but what if he's taken out of this world while on the grind. He tells me most things, but not all, I don't think.

From here, I will let Booker T. tell his story of the streets in his own cold words.

Part: Two

Booker T. Cold Ass Words

And He Got Bitchies

#.1 <u>Kim</u>

Meet Kim, the best hoe I got makin three stacks a night up here on 161, she ran that shit. I worked her seven days a week because her man had to have his money. She had no problem suck'n, fuck'n, lick'n or eaten just so long as you got some money. She told me she was 11 the first time her daddy sold that ass to his friend for fifty dollars. Afterward the man walked out of her room, her daddy walked in and handed her ten dollars. What type of shit was that, her own daddy sold her? Deadbeat mother left her with that dog of a daddy at age nine; he did a good job until that night. After that night she sold her own ass and there was no free fucks coming from that pussy not even for her own daddy, he had to pay too. As time went on for Kim out on the street, the ugliest shit happened to her. She felt a dirtiness that devour her mind most days. An adequate amount of dope used daily by Kim stopped that pain so she could keep up the good work.

I found Kim at age 37 seated in the bar on Hudson and Seventeenth. Fresh out of a treatment center she had a glow on her face that showed how good she felt about being clean. As I entered the bar, our eyes locked on to each other. Instantly, I could tell she had begun to melt. She could not stop staring at me nor could I stop checking her. The more I looked the more I knew she was mine. It took some time for me to work my way through the crowd over to her as I stopped to talk to every

other person grabbing hold of me in the place. It was as if everybody knew me that night or I knew them. I knew she had to have noticed the people with me. As I talked, we both looked at her as if I had questioned them about her. Finally, I stood beside her and could not help but see her shaking with lust. Shit, I bet myself that her pussy juices were running for me right then. I introduced myself then asked if she was there with someone. She tried to act cool while she looked straight in my face into my sweet brown eyes then softly answered *"Naw"*. I leaned my face close to her ear and said *"I'm digging you"* as I removed her left hand off her lap to lead her out to my car. I felt her heart was jumping, pounding hard as fuck through her hand while she followed me out to my bright red, Road Masters Deluxe Buick. I opened her door and she got in.

After we sat nice and comfortable with some smooth jazz, I started to spit my game.

Question, *"U got a man."*

"Naw"

"R you look'n for a man"

"Yeah"

"*Aright*, well I got a wife, so know that I'm not look'n for, another one. I am not looking for any pussy because my wife already got one of dem. What I need is some money and if it don't make dollars it don't make sense. Do you understand what I'm talkin bout?"

Before she could say yes, "Beep, Beep" my two-way sounded out so I answered.

My other bitch's voice said,

"I got two hundred for you daddy and I need some more of them things." My response

"I'm on my way" I started up the Road Master and pulled out from the curb as we traveled down the street I undid my jeans and pulled out my dick as I said *"Show me what you work'n with."*

Immediately her head went down and did not come up until her mouth was full. By the time we reached my destination, I let, Kim know I was happy with her. I then pulled up to a boarded up house and my girl came out handed me a large ball of money held together by a rubber band. I reached under my seat removed a package and handed it to her.

[80]

The two of us never spoke, she turned and walked away and I pulled off. Kim watched me as I drove down Main Street to the hotel where she fell fully in love with me. I left her with her pussy jumping like crazy and she been get'n my money ever since. Kim and I had only one misunderstanding on a night she came on her period .She didn't feel like working called and told me how she felt about not working. Before we hung up the phone, I stood in her hotel room asking her if she was sure, she can't work. The look in my eyes was cold; before she could, give me her slow ass answer I snatched her by her long blond hair, and dragged her white—ass, across the floor over to the bed kicking. Next I pinned her down on the bed, ripped off her underwear, then shoved my dick up in her ass with a gob of spit and dry fucked her hard in that asshole as she screamed,

"*Please don't baby please Booker T. I'll go to work.*"

There was nothing that bitch Kim could do but cry. As she sobbed, I fucked her until I came. After I got off that asshole, I said,

"*Get me a towel and clean me off!*"

She was shaking as she did as I ordered, partly from the sex, because chicks like that shit and partly out of fear, but she took her sore ass to work.

We never ever had a misunderstanding after that day. Some days I take her clothes shopping then out to dinner and not to a fast food place but to a fancy place where I had to make reservations. Although there are days she has told me she wishes she were my wife instead of Tweet. I even had Kim over to the house to meet Tweet and Tweet liked her. Shit, we all have done three way sexes. Nevertheless, she knows she will never be the wife I came home to every night. Hell, I would for sure half to be dead or in jail not to go home every night to Tweet. Still Kim always tells me she wishes it were her I was coming home to. Often she told me "Booker T you're the air I need to keep living with out you my life would be over." C she stop smoking crack and stayed clean for me, even though she was selling it for me everyday. That's right she sold pussy and crack because her man had to have big money.

Dominic

A dime piece white girl with long black hair draping down her back, stopping at the top of her phat-ass booty, I kept her around me for fun; I truly enjoyed her innocence and her whip (car). Her real name was so white girlish that she changed it to fit in with the black girls at her school. She was seventeen years old the daughter of a doctor. Dominic was so dumb and confused about life that she makes me laugh throughout the day. Dominic got the latest model Mercedes, just a little something from her grandmother who was a corporate lawyer. The girl comes from money, big money, but she was a tad dinghy in the head.

(How did we meet?) Well one night while I was sitting at the stop light on Livingston, a silver Mercedes pulled up beside me and started revving its engine like the driver wanted to race. Booker T. aint no coward, so I did the same with my engine, when the light changed the two cars sped off. It was close, but the Road Master was no match for the Mercedes. At the end of the race when the two cars slowed down, Dominic lowered her dark tinted window, and offered the loser a drink. I accepted under the condition that I get to drive the Mercedes. This was the start of a nice friendship. Although I

[83]

hated the fact this young-ass-bitch, really, aint got no money to put her hands on right now, but one day she will. The code was "If it don't make dollars, it don't make sense." There was no money for me to get from her, and she too young to fuck, but I loved driving her whip. I drove her car so much it felt like it's my own shit. After a while, dudes' started to think the silver Mercedes was mine.

"Booker T. why you never try to fuck me? Aint I pretty enough? Or you just don't like white girls?"

"Hey baby girl, you know you one fine ass white girl, with that pop bottle shape, but your jail bait to me. Just get older; I got you, you feel me? Until then you keep that pussy tight for me. I told you if I hear of you given my pussy away, you gonna disappear and no-one will find Yo ass.

She likes when I talk to her likes that, calling her bitches, but then she put on the sad eyes as I continued to talk,.

"Every one in this world has their time to shine. Moreover, when I say shine I'm talking about them doing what they do best. Kim sells pussy for me and Vicky sells my dope and you, well all I want you to do is keep looking good when you're with me, that's what you do best. You got it?"

Slowly she said, *"Yes, I got it."*

She sat quiet for some time as I drove the Mercedes up passed my strip joint to see whose car was in the parking lot. Cool, two of my Niggah's, LiL Don and Tiny's car are in the parking lot. Before I could decide to keep chilling with this bitch or go hang with the boys Dominic starts talking stupid again.

"So tell me Booker T. what your wife do, that's so great?"

My foot hit the brakes and my hand opened the car door as I said,

"*Hoe, hold the fuck up, what my wife does and don't do aint none of your business! I tell you what little girl; I'll call you when I'm ready to see you again.*"

The car door slammed hard showing my dislike for her and her car after I got out. With my back turned to her I never stopped walking away heading to the strip joint. Dominic sat in the passenger seat waiting, thinking I'll come back, and more so not believing I just got out and left the car in the middle of the street like that. She climbed over into the driver seat with tears filling her eyes. After a line of cars blowing, honking and shouting dumb bitch while they drove around her car. She knew she had fucked up with me and she probably wanted to call me, to say, "*I'm sorry, please forgive me*" but she knew that would set me off even more. The best thing to do was, to take her ass home and wait by the phone.

If I had one thousand, it would not be enough for me.

Booker T.'s club

"Hey Book, I saw you still fuck'n wit dat little white bitch. What cha need to do is let me suck that big pretty brown dick of yours." I stopped movement and just looked at the woman that spoke to me.

"Infinity, look at me, do I look like I'm in the mood for jokes?"

"Jokes! Jokes niggah I aint joke--n, shit I'm dead serious!"

I laughed, in a condescending ton *"Ha, ha"* thinking this should piss her off and get her out of my face for tonight. As I looked at the young woman I started, to reflect on her, damn my girl Infinity has been working at my club for some years now. I remember when she was a household name to many men in this city. Except for me, she is just my employee. Look'n at her sad ass then I felt kind a bad for her, because she used to be one of, if not the coldest, bitches in the city. That day, I had to be honest and say she aint nothing more then a powder head, what a damn shame, anyway.

"Where in the fuck do you think you goin'? Your shift aint over yet!"

"I'm going to get me some money, Aint nobody in there but Don, Tiny and LiL J and they don't fuck with me."

[87]

"Damn Fin, that's fucked up you can't get any money.

All right go home and I'll see you tomorrow."

"Alright Booker, I'll see you."

"Hey Infinity."

"Yeah."

"Here, take this." I peeled off a couple of one hundred dollar bills and handed them to her. *"Thank you daddy, you're a life saver."*

I stood there for a second to make sure she got to her car ok. As I walked into the club, I could still hear horns blowing at that dumbass still sitting in the middle of the street *"What a fucking idiot."*

The sound of the opening door had Tiny look around from behind Angel's fine ass and ask,

" Aye Booker T, what up my niggah?"

I locked the door behind me after I saw LiL Don stretched out on my damn pool table with one on his dick and another on his face. Does that motherfucker even know how much it will cost to clean that table? I got three pool tables, standard size, five soft butte chairs with a little table spaced out on the floor for lap dances. The dance poles shot up out of the bar counter one at each end of the bar. The girls can see their every move in the wall mirror that sat behind the bottles of alcohol. Door cost to enter is ten dollars and then all drinks cost five dollars a glass. I make some big money at this bar on the weekends. When I looked at Poor LiL J, who appeared to be getting straight molested by the new girl Tanya, damn all this fuckin' goin on and I can't think of nothing but pulling this hit on Fat Daddy with Tech.

"Oh baby that's my spot, don't, you about to make me cum!" Tiny moaned.

"Wow, ya'll too off the hook for me," I shouted before telling my help behind the bar. *"Yo, I'm going up to my office to do some paperwork make sure those men pay up after they're done. I don't need my girls going home unhappy."* While handing the bartender my .45 I looked through the mirror at the live sex show going on and for a second I was able to take my mind off the up coming job.

"Booker you alright baby?"

"No, but I will be, ah don't forget to send them up and call the girls a cab."

"Ok."

Peachey, that's my bartender's name, she about getting the money and she

[89]

don't take any shit so I hope they don't trip, because she won't hesitate at all when it come to busting that .45.

I walked up the steps, down the hall, six steps to the wall. There to the left of the door was an electronic pad 11251 turned off my alarm so I could enter my office it was half the size of a loft apartment. My corporate size tan desk sat across from the door. I took the remote from the desk to turn on three security screens inside my office. With the press of a button, I can focus in on the area or sound. From here, I'm able to see and hear everything that goes on inside and outside the club. Right then I needed to see the parking lot maybe, Tech was there. No, he was not there however; the gang would be up soon so I checked the small bar stocked with non-alcoholic beverages for ice. I love the place the way Tweet fixed it up, with the high gloss wood stained floor over at my office area. Then she placed gold carpet on the other half of the floor with a tan leather couch and love seat. Large diamond shaped marrows across the left wall and bay windows are along the right. In the middle of the floor, a large round table trimmed in gold to match the large picture frames trimmed in gold, of Tweet our children and myself.

Knock, Knock, Knock, snapped me out of the trance to look at the screen over my door. Don, Tiny and LiL J, I walked over and opened the door. As they came in, I could see that Don was wearing a vest under his jacket. I closed the door behind everybody, and sat on the edge of my desk waiting while everyone fixed a drink. After the guys fixed their drinks and

[90]

talked about their little freak fest we all took our seats at the table. Here we sat for a moment not saying a word. We just looked at the each other and the two empty seats. A few weeks had past since Kid got knocked and Roy started using dope again, and we don't know who would take over Kid's area until he gets out.

Bang, Bang Don hits the table with the handle of his 357 revolver.

"Now, we know the rules, guns on the table, gentlemen."

With that, we began the meeting. It went on for hours but as always we made the changes we needed to make and everybody went back to work. I watched the cameras to make sure they were gone before I started cleaning up.

"Beep, Beep, Beep..."

I looked at the monitor over my door to see who it was at my office door, standing there looking up at the camera was Angel with nothing on but a pair of heels and a pretty ass smile. The phone rings. It's Vicky. She got some money for me to come and pick up.

Knowing I have to go get that money left me stuck looking at her standing there.

"What am I doing? I can't just leave her standing in the hall, ass naked. I mean I am a gentleman."

I open the door and as soon as our eyes met, we just went at it.

Angel dropped down right there in the doorway and started undoing my zipper. Before I could say a word, she had my dick inside her mouth sucking the fuck out of it. From there I fucked Angel on my desk taking time to work on her nipples but she grabbed my head letting me know she wanted me to eat some of that pussy. Too bad, there aint but one pussy I will eat, and that is Tweet's. Her stuff tastes so fuck'n sweet all the time. Thinking about eating Tweet's pussy turned me into a lunatic so I fucked Angel on every piece of furniture in the room. We finally ended up in the middle of the floor, breathing hard and sweating.

"You fucked the shit out of me, baby." Angel said while gasping for air. *"Damn! It's been a minute since we've had a fuck session; we need to have more..."*

Even though I was tired and wore out, I rolled over and got up off the floor before I said,

"Look, Angel please do--not start."

"No I'm just saying' you could spend a little bit more time with me and your son."

"Wait what do you mean? I take good care of my son."

"I know, but I just want us to spend time together as a family."

"We do spend time together, we go out to eat, to the movies, skating, school plays, fun parks; damn what more do you want from me?"

"I want you to leave Tweet and be with me!"

"I aint never leaving Tweet. Bitch are you crazy or are you sick? Wait! Didn't you just fuck my homeboy earlier?"

"Yeah, but..."

" But what, bitch? Get out 'fore I smack the shit out of Yo stupid ass."

If I had billions, it would not be enough for me.

Vicky

My girl sat on the corner of Main and Kimble everyday and all through the night, hoping someone would stop and trick with her. Her clothing wasn't the best, her chest built flat like a boy, and there was no plump ass. Her skin shade, African black and hair matches the skin nasty as fuck. She looked a hot mess and not one car ever stopped to buy pussy from her.

Then I pulled up in that pretty ass Road Master and asked, *"Did you eat today?"*

She shook her head, no. Truth be told, she looked like she had not eaten for days. I ordered her to get in my car to go eat with me.

While we traveled, I Asked, *"When's the last time u ate?"*

She told me, *"Two days ago."*

I gasped the words out, *"Two days ago! What the fuck are you trying to tell me? You aren't gettin' no money out here, Vicky?"*

"I'm telling you I sit on that same spot all day everyday and not one car has stop for me."

[95]

"Okay, well I can see why you're having trouble with this line of work. Everybody aint made for hoeing and you really aint got a lot to work with. Like it or not that was the truth."

We pulled up to a late night eatin spot on the north end of Columbus.

I told her, *"Move your ass, girl; let's go eat."*

I opened my door and walked to the diner door, and she trailed behind, admiring my walk and the smoothness of my step. All chicks do it, and then tell me it looks like I'm walking on air when I walk. It's because I hold a confidence within myself that shows on the outside of my body. After I sat down in my seat, I did what all pimps do and crossed my leg. Vicky laughed and said; you did that as those pimps I've seen in movies do it. It was then I could tell by the look on her face she was thinking, *this muthafucka cold as ice and he got me with him, why?*

The woman took our order and while we waited, I asked her if she wanted to make some money for us. She would be sellin' crack out of an abandoned house. She sat and thought on what I was proposing, and then the food came to the table. While we ate, I continued to talk to her, but my pimp ton was harsher.

"Bitch it aint like you making big money sellin' ass. Shit, you stick with me and you can eat like this every night, hell you be the one pay in' for the food."

[96]

"What if I go to jail? You got me?" she asked.

"Little momma if u ride with me, I got u, going and comin'. Just remember, if it don't make dollars, it don't make sense."

That was how Vicky and Booker muthafuckin T came to know each other. I started her off with a teenager (sixteenth of crack) then I moved her up to a QT, (quarter ounce of crack) But, before we went there, I had to make her truly believe if she had fucked up my money I would have found her and killed her ass. Thus, I spent the slow money week with her allowing her to hang with me and chill. Call it, "get to know each other time" or that is what Vicky thought; but I was on some hunt a motherfucker down shit. I knew it was just a matter of time if I spent sometime in the area, the bitch I was looking for would show up. It was a chilly night for the end May, but Vicky and I sat at the bus stop on Cleveland and Mayo Street. Laughing and joking hard when I heard a voice that prompted me to look up at the very bitch I was looking for. When she saw it was me, Booker T, the man she owed and had been hiding from, her body made a jester to run, but by then I had my hands on her and she was not running anywhere.

"Booker T. please, please,"

Vicky not knowing what was going down had jumped up and stepped to the side.

"Hi Lisa, never thought I'd see you here, but now that I have, do you got

my money?"

Lisa shook her head, *"No."*

"No, well do you got my dope?"

Again, she shook her head, *"No."*

"No! Mmmmmm well I did tell you what I would do if you fucked up did I or did I not?" As I spoke, I placed my free hand inside my coat to my inner pocket and removed the set of small tin cutters. I kept them inside of a freezer bag for times like this. As I did so, I talked soft-like to Lisa.

"So, Lisa we did agree on three fingers as payment to me if you fucked up right."

This time Lisa nodded her head, *"Yes."*

"Okay, so today will be payday for me, do we agree on this?"

Again, Lisa agreed.

"Okay you chose to fuck up, so I will choose the fingers. I would like both thumbs and one ring finger."

I felt Lisa's shoulder tensed up, prompting me to get a tighter grip on her.

I began to use the ten cuter on her left thumb right at the joint. She screamed a bloody scream. I shoved a washcloth from my back pocket into her mouth to bite down on. Lisa bit and I cut. Vicky offered up her own shoestrings placed them tight on Lisa's wrist. Can't have her bleed to death now can we. Quickly I removed all three fingers, placed them in the freezer bag.

As Lisa set shaking in pain, I told her,

"Whenever she gets my money, you can get her fingers back!"

As I walked away with Lisa's fingers, she remained seated at the bus stop. I did call for help. Neither Vicky nor I spoke as I took her home. As she stepped out of my car, I asked here if she understood why I did what I did to that chick.

She nodded, *"Yes"*.

I then asked would we have the same problem.

She nodded, *"No"* before she closed the car door.

You the reader may feel I am a heartless individual and that I did Lisa wrong. That she did not deserve that type of treatment. Well I would like to go on record stating I'm not heartless but the game is. Moreover, Lisa and I played the game together and she acquired the pungent part of the game. Neither of us was triumphant, I lost money and dope, while she lost three fingers. The thing about Lisa was she had got so numb off the over use of crack her brain, her body and emotions' were shot down, no they where shot off while I cut her fingers off. It is depressing to know Lisa will still find away to light up her lighter to smoke her crack without the fingers.

Now on the first of the month I gave Vicky a whole loaf (ounce). That money flowed to her and she grooved out of three different abandoned houses. I switched her off and on all month to throw off the po-po.

When the money moved slower, I'd called her to say, "Put a hold on everything, get dressed cause we go'n out."

She and I hung at the Six Ball, shooting pool all night after eating dinner. I never have asked her for sex, but I did hold her in my arms. When she was going through the loss of her grandmother, I was there. I drove her to DC, paid for all expenses, and put money on her grandmother's headstone.

Journal **3**

Damn, Mr. Journal if I did not have you to talk to on these late nights I would go crazy. Stuck here full of a mixture of feelings, sadness, hatred and loneliness because I miss my husband and son so, so, so--much. Booker T has been gone two years now, my son two and a half years. I send big butt photos, and money but I feel it aint enough. When Booker T. first started to get locked up we were not concerned, it was State shit, he floated with no ops that aint shit. Then they stopped him, after he left a place with a new pack of dope and a gun. That too was state. Then the Fed's got onto his case and shit changed. My hate for the marked man has consumed my inner self to a drive to kill him.   Mr. Journal, I saw how much this fucka likes chicken. Every night 12:15, he has stopped at the chicken joint, over on Joyce Street. He sucked on them bones until 1 AM. He must have had hot sauces the way his ass gets back into his car headed deeper up north to a dope spot on Cleveland and Hudson. He enters the place for about 20: minute then on to the corner of 4th and 11^{th,} quick stop at the store, where he got scratch offs. He sits in the car for 15: min scratching tickets, if he got a winner, back into the store he goes. Next stop the titty bar where he sits in the parking lot for at least 15 minute, He got business going on down in his lap. Next, he goes in for one hour then back to his car. Next stop 4th and 17th drop spot he was in there for one hour.

When he leaves there, he takes a girl with him, and they ride around for half hour while she gave him a head-job. He takes her back to 4th and 17th. The titty bar just may be the spot. Now I need to pick what I will use to kill him. I can't use a gun, to much noise and mess. A knife, that's an up close thing and I would love to stick that thing up in him while looking him in the eye. Sounds good but I must remember I am a woman going up against a man. It will not be easy for me to keep the upper hand. I have to do more research on this.

Da third to go

Tiny, what can I say about my dude? His height looked to be six foot three, weighing around two hundred and eighty pounds. Yes Tiny is a big man with an even bigger heart. He was the only one out of our pack that got high damn near every day. He too would stop at the recovery club, because that was where his friends hung out; not because he wanted recovery. We rolled together and got money-shooting pool while he sipped his drinks on the north end to town. He would knock back all types of alcohol until he passed the fuck out.

Tiny's story maybe the simplest to tell; He had a wife, which just happens to be LiL Don's sister however, they aint together no more. I know everyone can relate to the word, <u>Divorce</u>. Ok, out of the marriage he got himself three kids. He referred to them as three grown ass kids that stayed with him in a two-bedroom house. He also had a crazy black chick he couldn't stand sleeping there in his bed. The two grown sons were 19, 18 and out of school with no job. One girl age 21 had two jobs, thus she had no time to care for her three-year-old son, who also lived at Tiny's house. Tiny, wasn't happy with his kids, nor did he like to stay in his own house. Tiny talked and talked about the shit he did not like but his big heart stops him from putting them all out.

[103]

He did tell the crazy black chick but she refuses to move and get the fuck on...

Most days he went home from work just to shout and yell. First, his two sons that had slept all day while he was at work. Then the crazy bitch would start her shit, because she wanted some dick and some money. The dick part was cool, but the money was out of the question.

I waited in my car one night while Tiny went into his house to get his pool stick allowed me to hear what I overheard,

"Tiny, what the fuck is up? I can't get no dick? You giving it all to that white bitch, can I get mine too muthafucka?"

The chick followed him back out to the car talk'n cash shit on him.

Then she said, *"Cool if you can't fuck me, I'll get someone else."*

Tiny laughed and said,

"Go 'head and take all your shit with you when you go, please."

Where Tiny was happiest at was across town, where he had this white girl that he wants in his house, but the crazy black chick just wont get the fuck on and out of the way. Thus, he paid rent on two cribs. Oh yeah, this dude had a little money, however, it just wasn't enough.

He had seven years in working for the State of Ohio's Sanitations Department; making good money, he wanted more money. He wanted some of the quick money his friends were getting. Tiny contemplated on how his will start his own thing purchasing some dope to sell. He went to LiL Don's crib on a Saturday, while Don and I packed some green beans (weed) for sale.

LiL Don's wife let Tiny into the house. Tiny spoke to me first. *"What up Booker T."* before he said, "Need a hook up, Don. What you want for a half of hard {half ounce of crack)? And do me right niggah!"

 LiL Don looked up as he said, "I got to say eight on that man {eight hundred} but, I could just give you one and you bring me back fourteen on it."

 Tiny laughed aloud and hard then questioned me, "Aint that some bullshit, Booker?" I had no answer for him.

Stillness hit the room before Tiny spoke with a deep harsh tone to Little Don.

"Get the fuck--out of here niggah! Do I look that stupid, to you?"

While he headed toward the door Tiny talked more.

"Look man, I aint about to work for you, or let you work me. I can get my

[105]

shit elsewhere, dude. I got love for you, man, but you aint right!"

LiL Don's face got that stupid look now.

Then Tiny said, "While I'm keeping it real with you, I'll put this shit out here too, how fucked up, I think that was, the way you did Kid on his money. I got to go. Get up with you later, man." There was nothing LiL Don could say about that last statement, because he knew Tiny was right. Tiny then turned, looked at me and asked, "Booker T., how in the hell you fuck with this dude?" I never answered.

Tiny went out LiL Don's door. Tiny's next payday took him on a trip out of town to his home city—Chicago. With his package, Tiny quickly blew up in the drug game, got two new cars, diamonds and gold, big time. Then, he and LiL Don went into competition. Customers looked for good ass dope for a low price. Tiny sold powder, hard, weed, and all types of pills; the same as LiL Don's did. As for me, I found myself in the middle of two one-time friends and in-laws. Tiny held down the North end of Columbus with the help of my crazy ass. Now don't get it wrong, the pack still hung out together at the strip club and other places, but the vibe just was not the same when we all got together. Tiny and I shoot pool all over Columbus for money against other dudes. As two of the biggest niggahs in a bar full of people, no one went up against us. However, I did have the chance to beat the shit out of two motherfuckahs about my money twice. Soon I got that name suspect, because I'm suspected of doing whatever the fuck I felt like doing at any time. LiL Don felt some type a way about me hanging' with that drunken ass niggah, Tiny. He called me to his house more than once to talk recovery on a deep level, reading the recovery textbooks with him to keep us powered. See, not only am I the youngest in the gang, but I had the least amount clean time, one year clean, and if my young ass goes back out to getting high, everyone would be hurt. In giving me the juice of recovery, he re-awakened it within himself. I was eager to get money without the use of drugs and I knew my wife, car, money and self would be lost if I got high on my own supply. I have no plan to go out like a sucker this time. I've tried to show loyalty to LiL Don, but I got a better deal with Tiny. Some days I just did not want to pay LiL Don's high ass prices, so I did business with Tiny, LiL Don's a money-grubbing muthafucka and it was hard to fuck with him all the time. The gang code was "If it don't make money, it don't make sense." The real story about LiL Don was, if he don't make more money than you, it don't make sense.

Tiny's Beat Downs

The first robbery on Tiny was a home invasion; no one was home but him. The day after the robbery I saw my man with a fat ass lip and I wanted to know what the fuck had happened. He told me how at 10pm someone knocks at his door, awakening him off the couch; it was light Outside when he had fallen of to sleep. He was still half-asleep when he started across the floor to open the front door. First, he hit the light switch on the wall next to the door, because the room was dark. Without looking first, Tiny opened the door. With swiftness two niggahs, shoved in through the door. They were on Tiny like water. They shoved him back onto the couch, all the while knocking him in the head repeatedly with guns. One with a .38 and the other man had a .45.

All Tiny could do was shout, *"Oh, lord please, please don't,"*

The last dude to enter went back and closed the door as the other dude asked,

"Who here with you in the house?"

"No-one-man! No-one!"

[108]

Tiny did not know who was there inside the house; he was drunk when he came in. While one dude continued to pin him down, he heard someone run up the steps, which set to the left of the front door. Up on the second floor, at the top of the steps sat a small box shaped area, the bathroom, to the right sat a bedroom door, and to the right again faced a second bedroom door. Tiny lie still pinned down by the gunman while he heard his belongings tossed about as they hit the floor. Tiny's heart did leaps inside of his chest with fear. He felt the knots on his head rise with pounding pain. Then, dude shouted down from up stairs

"I can't find nothing! Get that niggah talkin'!"

Bam, the gunman hit Tiny again, this time in the face hard. He felt his lip split. Tiny got out an Mmmmmm, before the gunman said,

"The sooner we get it, the sooner we leave, bitch!"

Tiny knew what they wanted so he said, *"It's down stairs in the basement!"*

The gunman called, *"Basement, bro."*

Dude ran down from upstairs and all three went through the dining area on to the kitchen and down the steps to the basement. In the large basement, Tiny went straight over to the washer, leaned it back, reached up under it and took out two large zip-lock freezer bags. One bag was full of money in

20s, 50s, and 100s and the other full with large rocks from nine ounces of freshly cooked crack.

As he passed over the goods the one robber with the 45 gun said, "This here isn't personal, man, but if you want to make it personal we can, and I'll kill your ass right here and now."

Tiny responded; while he touched his lip *"No, I understand it's business."*

The men took off up the steps and out of the house, with Tiny left in pain. His head and lip was hurt, but his pride was hurt more. He lost all the dope he had at home and all his money.

He did make a comeback off the dope and money he had out on the street. He and I talked about all the cribs we had run up into in the past and how he can't be slipping like that again. Tiny got his money back up fast, but he started to act stupid. The way he did business out in the open while, he sat in his car. He served out of his car as if it was legal. Weed, rock and powder he kept in his car while he got drunk in the bars. A number of times the car window was broken out all his work took and Tiny acted as if he did not care. Then Tiny received a bad beat down right in front of LiL Don's house one night. LiL Don never heard a thing Ha! This ass kicking took him to the hospital for five days near death. While I sat with him the first day, he told me what he was able to remember about that night. It was after my club had closed and we were going to hang out and shoot some pool. However, I took too long counting money the girls turned in. Tiny jumped into his car and started driving home as best he could with all he had to drink. At some point, he remembered LiL Don had call earlier that night requested to see him. It was three or four AM when Tiny's drunken ass made it to LiL Don's house, parked, and got out of the car. Before he could close the door, someone hit him from behind with something hard. He was not clear where they came from or how many there were. He went down on one knee, they hit him again, down on the ground he went, and feet started to come at him from all sides. All he could do was ball up to protect his face and chest. He felt someone dig into all his pockets. His keys snatched out of his hand, as he lies there hurt he heard his car drive off. This hit hurt Tiny to the point that he couldn't let anybody work for

[111]

him on the street. He needed every dime himself. He let go of the house his grown ass kids and that crazy chick had. Next, he had to sell two of his cars just to stay up. Yes, Tiny was doing badly! Next, police started to fuck with him, but all he had on him was some green beans and that was a misdemeanor. His end of the road came with the police stopping him on Broad Street, inside his car was 72 grams of crack and a 9mm. The ugly white bitch got him out, but two days later he found himself pulled over again, he had 38 grams of hard and a 9mm with hollow tips in his car. He got out again on a future indictment free for three weeks and then the Feds came, about five in the morning, surrounded his house and took Tiny and the white girl off to jail. While he sat in jail, the white girl got out and continued to stand by her man. She went out and got a marriage license and they got married. Yes, he got married just in case the Feds have conjugal visits time once a month. My boy Tiny will be free in 2015.

Da Forth to Go

Jimmy, A.K.A. {LiL J}

I developed an interest in Jimmy during my mandatory 90 meeting within 90 days of recovery. I listen to him talk about how he got into this recovery world. His story was mine and that fascinated me. After the Saturday 3 o'clock meeting, I introduced myself to him. We talked one-on-one over coffee and quickly we became friends. He and I shared damn near the same get high stories. Jimmy told me how he started out on the streets of New York at age twelve as a crack dealer. An old school dude he hung with placed the name, LiL J, on him. As I listened and watched him, the Lil J in him began to come forth.

Lil J told me by age fifteen he grew a crack appetite that drove him to sleep in abandoned houses or on the streets inside of a box. His habit started with joints of weed. Then, he heard how nice the high was with crushed crack and weed mixed in a joint plus how that shit provided a five-hour get-high. Lil J tried the mix, and liked it! With the crack mix, he smoked less often and was able to function better. See the weed high made him sleep after eating and he missed money, because he was unable to make deliveries. However, the mixture made him mellow he could think and get that money.

After a number of months smoking the mix of weed and crack everyday, he ran out of weed. That stopped the mix and fucked his early day get high routine. He called everyone he knew that sold weed and found talk of a drought. No one had weed for sale. He wanted to get high so bad that he got a tall can of Red Bull. Nevertheless, it did not give the high he was looking for. He felt pissed having the crack without the weed. Nevertheless, his crack sales were bang'n and he stayed on the love for the money. As he delivered his crack, he inquired about weed, but crack smokers knew nothing about weed. Lil J noticed the pipe in use at every sales stop. That white smoke flowed through the glass pipe so nicely. He decided to try a pipe full of crack.

"Hey, let me try that thing."

Six words he now wished he had never said!

The houseman, reluctant about helping someone with that first hit said, *"Ok, here you can use this pipe,"* as he offered up a pipe to Lil J, who had a glow of joy on his face.

He took the pipe then asked, *"How you do this thing?"*

The houseman took the pipe back then placed a nice size piece of crack on top of the pipe. He then used a yellow lighter to melt the crack some. All the while explaining, *"I do this so the crack won't fall off, when you hold it like a cigarette to your lips."*

With the pipe set and ready for smoking, he passed it back to Lil J. The houseman asked one more question of Lil J before the lighter went up to the pipe,

"Are you sure you want to do this, dude?" With his lips wrapped around the glass pipe, Lil J nodded his head yes!

The houseman began to teach, "Ok, as I hold the fire here at the end of the pipe, you inhale the smoke through, into your lungs slow and steady, then hold the smoke in as long as you can."

With great anticipation, Lil J gazes at the fire at the end of the pipe then did as he was told. He pulled in the smoke and held it until he became light-headed. He closed his eyes feeling that good feeling, but still held in the smoke. He felt his body tingle all over then he heard church bells ring inside his head loudly" Bong, Bong" at ten o'clock at night. The next thing he felt was his dick get hard and jump up and down. He grabbed it with his left hand, still holding the pipe with the right hand. He slowly exhaled the smoke as his eyes popped wildly open. Still holding onto his dick, he

[115]

felt like he was ready to fuck! He had a true hunger for some freaky sex and the ugly, funky girl there at the house worked out ok for him.

Lil J's first hit of the crack pipe allowed obsession and compulsion to take over his life. As he tried to hear the bells ring, again he smoked up all his shit and everyone else's he could. He did not know! That first feeling was just that, the first! He can never get the first high back, but his desire to have it, took him to doing whatever! Wherever's mixed with hopes of him acquiring the same feeling with the bells—ringing loudly inside his head. Whatever's took him into Juvenile Court?

While on a court ordered drug treatment for the umpteenth time, Lil J learned more about the sickness he had called addiction. He learned how obsession was the never-ending thought of the crack. Damn! That shit called his name day and night nonstop. Compulsion was his actions the drive and the need for more of the dope once he had the first taste. An over whelming impulse he felt to do whatever he had to do for more dope. He understood it all starts inside his head. He tried to change his thoughts that moved through his mind. Lil J focused on his mother, whom he had not talked to since age twelve, when he left home. Each day clean, he learned more about his thinking and feelings disease called addiction. He had to understand that there was no cure for this sickness. The most hopeful aid against his sickness was abstinence from all drugs. Abstinence and only abstinence would help him never feel dope sick again. Then Lil J looked me in the eyes and asked me *"Booker T., you do understand that there is no cure?"*

I nodded my head yes before Lil J went on with his story. With my eyes fixed on him, I listened.

While his body and mind got strong, he felt an even stronger need to see his mother. After his time was up at the treatment center, it was back onto the streets of New York, for him. He had no home to go back to, so he stayed in a shelter. In the shelter, there was a lot of drug use. He felt he needed a change of location to have a chance at this stay clean one day at a time thing. It had always been impossible for him to stay clean there, so it was just a matter of time. Still enthusiastic with thoughts of seeing his mom, he visited the old neighborhood. He questioned many people that still lived in the area. Some knew of his mom and some did not but none gave help as to her whereabouts. His persistence to find her took him to knock on a door that turned out to be a cousin. They invited him into the house and offered him dinner. Over dinner, he found out *his mom moved to Columbus, Ohio.* Before he departed, he received phone numbers for family he had not seen for years and his mom. Over the next three months he made call after call reuniting with family. He and his mother talked almost every night. LiL J moved to Ohio into his mom's home to be closer to her.

[117]

Lil J was in a new city. Upon his arrival, he should have spent a day with his mom then he should have gone to a recovery meeting. He knew to look for people like himself to talk to if he had a growing feeling to get high. He learned in treatment that people, places and things would get him high again or they could keep him clean. After two weeks living with his mom, the get high dreams started hitting him hard. He awoke in a cold sweat, unsure if he did use dope again or had it been a dream. He had forgotten the part about recovery being an ongoing process. Everyday he must be working on recovery or he is working on a relapse.

There is no "I got time."

The hunger for one more get high is real inside of every dope fiend. An addict going to meeting and talking to other recovery people working on their recovery helps. Yes, it helps to keep the active drive/hunger or demand for one more use, arrested/locked the fuck away from the power to cause harm on self and others. Over time, Lil J did take notice of the drug activity in his area. He saw the hand-to-hand passing of the dope. Then it happened one day, he took the cut/back alley coming from the corner store. There it was a sack of the good shit on the ground.

The voice of cushion shouted inside of his head "*Keep walking.*"

Damn it, he did not listen. Instead, he listened to the other voice that said,

[118]

"Could it be? We better pick it up and see for sure. Ok. Now, we had better test it. O-yes, it is the shit."

If Lil J had an active working recovery program in his life, he would have never stop to question what it was. In short, he would not have cared.

He had a choice and made the wrong one. So once again, he did not stay clean. His mother had the rent money in her top dresser drawer. The word here is "Had." She was Lil J's first victim to help him continue to get high after the sack was all gone.

It pained his mother to say, *"Son, you got to go."*

Yes, she put him out of her home but what could she do.

Onto the streets of Columbus, he went to chase the dope again. A new city offered Lil J new people to fuck over and new abandoned houses to sleep in. Yes, everything truly was the same except the city, this city offered less abandoned houses for people like Lil J to live in. However, it did offer plenty slow dope boys for him to catch off guard. Ohio dope boys knew zero about how a fiend like Lil J scope game for hours at a distance while he examine every move that went down. One crack dealer had clocked money all day with his stuff stored inside of a brown bag. He left it on the ground a safe distance from him where he could see it. This worked if the police showed up; the crack's not on his person. Now, it is near dark outside and that dope boy can't see that well.

[119]

Lil J's heart pumped fast in the near dark! Faster then it had ever pumped here in this city. His body nervously bounced up and down, as he worked up the nerve to steal that dope. The dope boy just re-sat the bag down on the street and walked away, his back now to the bag as he walked over to where his friends stood.

The voice inside of Lil J head told him, "Do it, do it now!"

Lil J took—off—running, in a full gallop, blasting past the boy's back. He never stopped after he snatched the bag of dope up off the ground. His feet moved fast down the back alleyways from 22 and Mound over to the corner of Champion and Main Street. At that corner, he froze! His heart pumped so loud that he hears it throb out through his ears. He held his pose as still as a cockroach in fear of the approaching foot! Lil J had to be sure his pursuers were not in sight. This was not his first time doing this type of thing, but it would be his last, if they found him.

He whispered to himself, "The coast is clear."

He moved two more streets in stealth-fullness up to, 18th and Mound. His destination was an abandoned house on Parsons Ave. It still had water and lights and he called it home. While Lil J's movement slowed down with caution his heart kicked up pace from the approaching voices! He could hear the men as they shouted back and forth "Do *you see him*?!"

The loud talking closed in even closer. Lil J glanced about for a place to

[120]

hide. A boarded-up house stood in front of him. Only a half a sheet of wood covered the open door-way but the windows were fully covered.

He moved quickly, up to the door with prayerful words, "Please let me be able to dip into here."

His observation of the wood showed that some previous visitors had loosened the nails. His lack of food allowed his miniature body to slip right in with just the lift of the board. Lil J stepped inside just in time, before he overheard two men outside talking.

First, a deep voice said, "Fuck'n crackhead, man, we aint never gon' be able find that piece of shit."

The other voice sounded miserable when he said, "I know, man, but that one bag had 50, 20-dollar pieces in it, so I got to try something. Shit, it's my ass if I aint got dudes money in the morning."

Lil J's head tipped to the side now, as it had done that night so long ago. He showed how he focused his ears to listen to the men outside the house. I know just what he felt having done the same thing back in my own hometown. I felt deep intensity as I listened to him describe the death like pose he held. His back pressed tightly against the wall. Lil J thought he heard the dudes leave, but he still did not move. Repeatedly his mind whispered, "Ok light up now." However, his legs remained paralyzed with fear. After a short time of more silence, he did start to move with a slow side step. His back still press tight as hell up against the wall fearful someone may see him.

Then he laughed aloud as he said, "As if someone would see me through the windows, when they to had a board over them. Booker T. man I did the side step midway of the wall until I stepped into something mushy. That was that emotional shocker that UN froze my mind to preparer me for the new problem. The word, "Shit" slid from in between my lips. Damn! I knew what it was I stepped into, but I did not want to believe it."

Lil J stopped his words and took time to breathe.

Then he said, "I took out my lighter and flicked it as I bent down to get a close look at what I had on my open toe sandal shoe. Fuck, a pool of human shit dumped right on the floor and I stood in it!"

My own stomach dropped, sickened at the thought of that shit, because I have been inside of such a place and seen the same things. I listened more as he said he no longer felt concerned with who may be there. He was so sickened with shit on his foot and sandal. His consciousness of the smell of this house filled his nose and he needed a hit of dope. Right there and then he opened that bag took out his hitter and took a big blast.

Damn, this city was different, but the realities of getting high were the same. Once again, Lil J wore the same clothing day after day, smoking crack until there was none to smoke. He slept in dark places like this one here, only to awake lying next to a pool of shit and piss left by someone else. Once again he walked the streets in fear of someone fuck'n him up for the things he did the day before. This was Lil J's life until the age of eighteen. Whatever's took him to the adult Court system, where he received a choice: Recovery or Workhouse? He took the road to recovery; by the time, I got to the recovery world, LiL J already had eight years clean.

With eight years clean, my dude was a short good-looking brown skin man. He stood 5 feet tall, 155 pounds with a nice build. He no longer feared the dope man, but he had girl trouble on top of girl trouble. His weekly new girl in his bed came with drama. Women fought over him constantly, blamed babies on him and we know child support goes along with that shit. I even had the chance to sit in the hospital with him after one bitch stuck him in the back with a steak knife. His psycho bitch saw his truck drive into the motel parking lot on High Street so she followed. Not onto the lot, but she parked on the street and walked where she could see. As he stood in the lobby signing into a room with a girl, his psycho, full of rage rushed into the lobby and stabbed him once. It would have been more, but he quickly turned and knocked the shit out of her. No lie he knocked her all the way the fuck out. At the hospital LiL J found out, she nearly killed him with that knife hitting his left lung. When I got to LiL J's hospital room, he had two chicks in there with him. Chicks I knew he had banged before, and all three of them where laughing and playing about kicking old girl's ass for stabbed him. Before I left, he and I had time to talk alone.

I told him, "*Dude, you should be pimping, the way you stack bitches.*"

Lil J laughed then said, "*Man, I like pussy and getting head that is how I use a chick.*"

Out of the hospital grateful to be alive, he went back to doing the same shit, along with working on his dream of having a photo shop. Family photo for cash; and he had the chance to do the photo job, at the conventions. Okay, LiL J tried to hang with us, as if he is a big dog, but it was hard. His money never did stack up to ours. I understood when he took me to the side and said, "*Booker T., man It just don't feel right when everyone come out of pocket with a fat knot, and I can't. Even though you tell me, 'We got you, come on go with us.' It just aint cool for me. I have to get my own money up, dude. I feel I have to go hard to get that big money.*"

He stayed in the rooms of recovery with the rest of us, but he had a plan. He decided to take over the West End of Columbus. He went to LiL Don, hoping to keep the money inside the family/gang. I was there and seen the Lil Don talk that same dumb shit to LiL J. O-yes he tried to put a niggah to work for him. Lil J started out spending money with some-other dude back in New York. He had to go back to get his little girl from her mother who was on crack so bad she couldn't take care of her anymore. His daughter, aged nine, needed her father now so he did his buy of dope at the same time. Back in Columbus, he opened up three sets of traps {Dope house}. LiL J had it poppin on the west end. LiL Don and I stopped over to hang out with LiL J a bit just to see how a niggah put it down. I compliment, *"Man, this setup's sweet. I like how you got it."*

There were three houses side by side; the second floor bedroom wall connected the houses. The dope fiend will never enter the true door that the crack came from. The lay out was a fiend would enter the far left to cop their dope. A call was made for it and a person comes down the steps with the dope. The crack passed through the connecting walls. A large poster of a hot sexy chick conceals that hole. If the police came with a warrant for this house the fiends are entering, they will find no dope. He had a number of traps set up like that.

"Aint nothing, dude, just how we get down in New York, my niggah! *So, you trying to come and eat with me?"*

Before I could respond, LiL Don shouted out *"Hell no, he aint got to eat with you niggah! He got his own shit."*

I spoke up to cut into the bullshit, *"No LiL J man, I like it up North, I still make more money pushing hoes than crack, plus the hoes push the crack, too. Man, I'm good where I'm at, but if things change, I do know where to come."*

Everyone went back to work, me up north and LiL Don to one of his spots.

LiL J had only one problem at this time, how to deal with his daughter; she hated him and called him a hypocrite.

Often she asked, *"Daddy, how can you share the good recovery in the* recovery meeting and kill sick people like mommy everyday?"

She began to rebel in school, acting out, fighting, and getting poor grades. He didn't know what to do for her, but that was alright, because something was about to be done for him.

The Feds had him under surveillance for sometime so when he got sucked up, they had him, with taped voice recordings, video recordings of hand-to-hand pass offs, plus all types of guns came from LiL J's crib 9 mm, two mac 10's and sawed-off shotguns. LiL J's bust made the T.V. News and the Columbus Ohio press. Great minds think alike he will be going to the fed prison praying for a fuck day. In preparation, he also got married downtown at the county jail. The lucky one was a sweet chocolate lady he met in New York City at a 12-step meeting. After some years of dating long distance, she moved to Columbus to be with him. She fully understands she could become "Pussy on the shelf". However, she felt Lil J was worth it. As the wife, she has decided to care for her husband's needs and tend to his little girl until he returns in 2015.

Booker T. /A. K. A. Suspect

Today marks the new beginning of a new chapter in my life. Out of treatment one year and still clean, everything has been great, here in this new city. Got me a bad bitch and she's sharp as shit. She stopped her move and grove to trust in me to keep the money roll'n in like clockwork.

"What's up niggah, You *good?"* Tech questioned me as I awakened out of a trance.

"Yeah man I'm good, I'm good." His car had come to a full stop at our destination; I looked around to see if the vicinity was clear then I said, *"Time to get out."* As we did so I felt somewhat nervous, see this type of situation could get me killed. *"Damn its quiet as shit"* I whispered to Tech, while we creep down the sidewalk. This mark lived in one of the most prominent neighborhoods in the C.O. We walked up the driveway very slow and tried not to make any noise, except the ground was made of loose gravel. Then I started to think, *"What kind of bitch ass muthafucka won't even pay for a real driveway?"* As we keep it on the move, I glanced at Tech's face and I saw that he was scared out of his mind. I best get all the way into the game so I won't come up dead tonight. Shit it just may have been a better idea if I just go head and kill Tech then kill myself for even being out here with this bitch ass niggah! Okay, I noticed a light on in one of the rooms up stairs. If I were right, that would be his bedroom. As we got closer, I could hear the faint sound of moans. So far so good, everything was as planned.

Tech and I walked up to the front door were I saw what looked like one of those cheap home security cameras. Nevertheless, I'm not worried about anybody there to check us out, because the only person that could be looking was upstairs getting the shit sucked and fucked out of him by my girl Kim. We took one last moment to make sure every thing was every thing before we went inside the door. My hand went for the doorknob when Tech whispered,

"Yo, make sure your safety off"

It was at that time right there I decided I would kill Techs ass. I don't know why his act'n this way, but I can't take any chances.

I shot back in a low but sharp tone.

"My shit aint got no safety"

Again I reached out with my right hand while I held a sawed off double barrel shotgun in my left. Tech was behind me with his forty-five like he ready for anything even though I knew he wasn't. I turned the knob and sure, as shit the door opened right up. The words, (Damn that's my girl Kim) shot through with my mind with all the other many thoughts as we entered the crib. It's dark but because the street light came in the front window, I could see good enough not to bump into stuff. This place was huge on the inside some twenty five thousand square feet with a five-car garage and this niggah won't pay for a paved driveway.

"Tech you check around down here for the safe I'm going up top," I whispered and we split up so we could hurry up and get this money and get the fuck out of here while Kim had this dude's attention. At least that was what Tech thought. (See this whole time I'm on some murder shit.) Before I went upstairs, I stood and watched Tech for a few minutes creep-in further and further into the other room. I said to myself, *"Fuck"* as I saw how easily he moved around the room. Only a small area got light coming in from the front door and you couldn't see much of anything past the stairway and the entrance to the other room but the niggah must have had a candle stuck up his ass that shined light out his eyes or something because he could see in the dark. However, as for me on the other hand I knew ever inch of this house, thanks to the girl upstairs. See, Kim's one of my best hoes. This sexy white chick had tits size 38D that set up right in your face. She could turnout any bitch or niggah and break their asses like it aint nothing. My baby was born to hoe just as I was born to pimp. Too bad pimping aint my first love it's my second. My first love was robbing of big dope boys and that shit got me here tonight. Fat-daddy was one of the biggest dudes on the north side. He owns dope traps everywhere plus a nightclub, pool halls, after hour spots and a few car lots. Therefore, when I say that this was it, one of them very good hits, you know just what the fuck I'm talking about. I stood still in the big entrance area that gave way to the double staircase. Tech was out of sight and out of mind when I saw a crystal fountain in the middle of the two-way staircase that looked all bitch-e-fide. It had some kind of soft pink light behind it made the water look like pink lemonade. I never saw the fucker when we first came in

but that's ok. I made a mental note right there, (Do not forget to shoot the damn fountain! Yeah this bitch-ass dude has to die. It was hard but I snapped back to reality; this mother-fucking fountain had me pissed-off. I took two steps back from it, turned around to get the shit scared out of me. Tech dumb ass stood there with this big kool aid smile on his face. It was at that point that I realized that he seen the fountain privies to his journey into the other room and no doubt stood in there and laughed his ass off. He knew as soon as I seen that damn fountain I would become all psycho and he was right. For a second I stood there I had to smile myself, shit was funny. We nodded at the same time and started our adventure up the stairs. This place was built nice and solid so we could move along quickly. Tech walked on the left staircase and I on the right. At the top we moved slowly down the hall and made sure to stay in the middle do to the darkness up here we don't want to bump into anything.

"Ooh, shit damn bitch, tighter, tighter please," was what we heard, as we tipped closer to the only lit room in the hall.

"Tight; yes make it tighter bitch, ooh, ooh, oohs."

We paused and I whispered *"that aint no woman's voice."*

OH, SHIT!

"Damn Yo, was that Fat-daddy, I just heard?"

We moved up closer to the door and stood as we listened we began to laugh our ass's off. As we laughed, I turned the doorknob.

[131]

I didn't care that Fat-daddy heard us laugh or seen us in the doorway.

"Bitch! Get off me! Get the fuck off me bitch! You set me up. Untie me! Now!"

I opened the door in time to see my bitch Kim un-twist a coat hanger off that fat muthafucka dick. He enjoyed him self when Kim tied him face up spread eagle on the bed then twist a hanger tight around his dick un-till he shot cum everywhere. Tech and I walk on into the room into his eyesight. I said,

*"*Fat-*bitch, I mean Fat-daddy what's up bro?"*

When he looked up at me, he knew it was over. True fear filled his eyes as he attempted to scream for help. His mouth opened in time for the barrels of my shotgun. I rushed it into his mouth to muffle the full sound. He looked up at me with a look that I have seen time and time again. Even with tears of terror dancing from his eyes, I could tell he recognized me.

"I can just imagine what must be going though your head now that you see my face and know who I am. That also means you know what I'm capable of so don't fuck with me and I promise to kill you quick. Play and it'll be a long, slow, and painful night for you, your choice."

I said all that with no expression on my face or hesitation in my eyes. Kim had retreated and cleaned herself up, only to return to where she stood on the other side of the bed. I could see she was a bit fearful of witnessing what may go down here tonight. So, I told her to go look around for things out of ordinary. She knew just what I meant, did as I told her, and left the room.

"So Fat-ass tell me how we going to do this?"

I asked while I took the gun out of his mouth.

"Please man, please I'll give you any thing you want, please don't kill me

[132]

please. I won't tell anybody about this man," He then cried, *"I'll leave town and everything Booker man, please,"*

You know for about 30 seconds, I think that I believed him, NOT! Tech held no stomach for this type of shit and took a seat over by the door. He knew I was about to do some hurt full shit to Fats. There was an eerie silence in the room for a few seconds. Then it began. I walked over to a large china lamp unplugged it and firmly held it as I walked back to the bedside. Slam! I slammed it as hard as I could to fats head! Crash sounded the lamp as it busted into what seem like a million pieces. Blood splattered across the headboard and me. Fats laid there trembling from the pain and fear that rippled though his body.

"So Fats, about those keys, combinations, secret pass words anything? I got from now, until muthafucka.

I look back over my shoulder at Tech's expression on his face. Seated in the chair with the same big ass Kool-Aid smile made me to smile too. The sound of a bitch ass man blubbering snipped my head around. Then I said those last words to fats,

"O, hell no, don't start crying now bitch it's to late for that Yo bitch-ass need to start talking." After that, it was all work.

What felt like minutes, but had to be hours later, "*Yo! Yo! Yo! Hold the fuck up muthafucka! Don't you want to get in to at least one safe before you beat the niggah to death?*"

Tech butted into my obvious groove.

"*Yeah, Ok, you right, your right.*

Tech now stood at my side and said, *let me talk to him some.*

Shit, I was tired so I said,

Ok, well you talk to him I'm going to find Kim."

"*Why?*' Tech questioned as I moved towards the door.

"*Because she been gone to long* "

"*Ok, Ok*" Tech said as he turned his attention to fats and I walked on out the door

I over heard Tech began to ask for what we came for. As I walked, down the hall and listened for sounds of Kim's movement around the house. I heard a sound come from inside one of the other rooms. I paused, slowly reached around to my back and pulled out the big four-five. I moved toward the sound while bent down low then leaned in for a quick look. Damn what a pretty site, Kim was bent over the arm of the sofa to pick somethin up off the floor. My mind went blank and my dick got harder than a baseball bat. I stepped in to the room pulling out my dick yes it is suck-me, suck-me, time. I called to Kim,

"Here *baby come do daddy a quick suck.*"

The next sound wasn't the one I wanted but it did just fine. Tech had walked up on me with out me hearing him. Then after standing close but not to close, to me he announced,

"I got them"

Kim stood up; I turned and smiled while putting my dick away as we walked over to Tech.

Kim said, *"Well let's get the money and get the hell out of here,"*

I said. *"Ok, but before we go I got to kill Fats."*

Tech quickly announced, *done"*

With a tone of protest I questioned, "You *killed him already? Damn, I wanted to kill him"*

Tech held his kool-aid smile when "My *bad"* flowed out of Tech's mouth. Now I'm pissed as fuck so I tell him,

"Man just hand Kim the combinations so we can load."

She went though the house opened safe after, safe as Tech bagged up the money and drugged them to the front door. I loaded the bags into Fat's car I got from the garage.

"Are we done here?" I asked Tech

"Yeah we done" he responded.

"Alright get in and take the money to the spot I'm going to get the car and meet y-all there right?" I questioned

"That's what's it do," said Tech

[135]

Seeing Kim safe in the car with Tech I tapped on the roof and said,

"Good now go."

"What," said Kim as she looked at me with a frown on her face

"What are you gettin ready to do? Before I could say, anything Tech told her that I was going back in to shoot that pink ass fountain and pulled off leaving me standing in the driveway. I couldn't help but think to myself,

"Yep gona shoot me a fountain."

Then I turned around went back in the house while whistling the song to my favorite TV show Andy Griffin.

Hell no, Tweet at the Spot

The spot was a one-story building that once was a bar. The bar counter to this place was ripped out and left no trace of it ever being there. My husband Booker T. bought it to use for a hangout/ storage place. I put in a plush ass wall-to-wall tan carpet with large black leather furniture. I think the place looks good with the light brown wood panels on the walls.

"What's up my people?"

Shouted Tech as he dragged two moneybags into the Spot and over to the desk. Kim entered behind him and said not one word, but looked sad as hell. She journeyed over to sit on the floor in between my legs and put her face into her hands.

"What's wrong?"

I asked after I placed my right hand on Kim's head; she just shook her head while in a sweet quiet voice she said,

"Nothing I'm just waiting for Booker T. to get here, that's all."

Vicky dressed in a light grey Roca Wear sweat suit and a pair fresh forces, stood inside the stock room doorway before asking,

"Where's daddy at?"

I answered without taking my eye off the 77-inch plasma flat screen TV

"Your daddies on his way"

See me being Booker T.'s right hand and wife, I knew where he was most of the time. We have been together for some years, and its' well known that from the time we met until now the two of use are inseparable.

[137]

"Yah, Tweet," called Kim.

"Hey Kim, what's up baby girl?"

"Can I talk to you for a second Tweet?"

I sensed something to be severally wrong by the sound of Kim's voice. With out a delay I stood up out of my chair and reached down to give Kim a hand up. Still holding on to Kim's hand I lead her off into some other room while looking back at Vicky giving her a node and an eye contact that said you take care of out here until I get back. Vicky also knew by that look I had given her do not let no one disturbed me.

To keep Tech busy she did what any women would do in her position, she started to disrobe. It did not take long for her to stand naked. Vicky never did were underwear mainly because of her shape. No ass, no titties, shit why waste money on underwear, were her thoughts while she get dressed to leave the crib. This thing about her fuck'n Tech definitely won't be a problem, he'll stick his dick into any bitch he can. Yeah, that will work just fine with her, since it's been a few years since she last fucked. Tech was seated at Booker T.'s desk focused on the count of the money. The money looked so good he was oblivious to all other activities on the other side of the room. Vicky called to tech with a super sexy sound

"Tech, what cha do-in?"

While she slow stepped across the floor.

"What! Bitch, I'm counting money, damn can't you hear the money machine."

Vicky yelled back

[138]

"Who do you think you talking to like that, niggah?" She stopped movement toward him and just stood there. She knew Tech would look up now to see what the fuck she about. As she thought, he did look up. His next move was to drop the money and his paints. The two of them wasted no time Jumpin onto the black leather sofa, that sits at the end of Booker T.'s desk, where Booker T.'s money sits. As Tech fully un-dressed, he thought,

"Yep, come on and give that pussy. Oh yes, one day soon ,you and all this shit gone be-long to me and only me, Fuck Booker T. all this shit will be mine. Like Booker T. I'm going to be collecting from all you bitches and will be fuck'n Tweet and Kim at the same time, just like Booker T."

Tech situated himself on top of Vicky's hot ass body, but can't really start to enjoy himself, because the bitch aint got no titties or hair on her head, damn from the hips up she look like a dude. His brain kept shouting.

"Damn I can't fuck no dude, I aint gay! "

Therefore, he raised off and flipped Vicky on to her stomach, while telling her "Come *on put it out there. "*

He then grabbed her at the waste, with both hands, pulling her up to get her up onto her knees. One last command,

"Gone girl, get that dip in your back. "

He slid his dick, up into that tight pussy and the fuck'n started but it was not the good fucking Vicky expected.

This niggah continued to pull way--back as if he got a long ass dick. It kept falling out so he had to keep putting it back into the pussy. Tech's dick was fat but to damn short. She took no pleasure in this fuck at all, not that she was an expert on fuck'n. Although sex etiquette teaches, *"pray for a fast orgasm, so she can go and clown him to the other ladies."* He has a short dick and every female should know it.

Over in the other room two ladies sat on the some large box and talked.
"What's up Kim?"
"Tweet, you know I been with BookerT for sometime now and.
Before she could finish I cut in thinking I know what she would say.
"What; no wait, let me guess. You want a better car, more clothes, jewelry, and new furniture, Is that it Kim.?"
With an even sadder tone, Kim tried to speak up for herself.
"Hold on Tweet, I don't need anything new, and I love every thing about your husband. He treats me better than anybody, I have ever been with and you know that, so—why, you coming at me all fucked up?"
Now with my foot stuck in my mouth I had to say,
"All right Kim, your right, I shouldn't have snapped at you like that and I do apologize.
Before I said my next words, I got up, walked over to some other boxes, and opened it to look inside for the contents. Then I spoke with a soft voice,
" Ok, Kim what's up baby, let me know what's up with you?"
Kim had the sound of true depression in her words as she talked.

[140]

"First I know just like me you're worried about Booker T, because he's not back yet. But he's alright that much we can be sure of, but that's not what I needed to talk to you about."

As I listened, I became overly agitated with the bullshit of this whole conversation. Why this bitch playing words games with me was the question inside my head, I think she could see all that on my face when I nicely said,

"Please say what it is then!"

"It's Tech Tweet"

"What about Tech Kim?"

"I don't trust him Tweet I really don't"

"Why, has he said or did something behind Booker T.'s back?"

"No, it's nothing like that, plus he knows not to say shit about Booker around me."

"So what was it then?"

Now we are facing each other with eye-to-eye contact.

" Well I've been hoeing for along time, for the most part, I've been able to feel people out."

I came back with,

"Ok, The whole sixth sense thing."

"Right" Kim said,

"Well, what are they telling you?"

[141]

Is what I had to ask, because I'm clueless to where the fuck she going with this.

"Tweet, everything in me, tells me that we can't trust Tech."

"Are you sure?"

I questioned, because there just has to be more to what she's telling me then that.

"Yes"

"Well I must talk to BookerT. To see what he thinks, but in the mean time, keep watch on Tech, ok?"

"Ok"

As I start to reclose the box I opened, Kim called my name again.

"Tweet!"

"What Kim?"

Listen!

The two of us listened, and then Kim asked, "What's that buzzing sound?"

"Oh shit!

My cell phone

"Hello, hey baby"

I whispered back to Kim,

"It's Booker T."

"What cha doing Tweet?" He asked

"I'm just chilling, waiting on you baby"

"That's what's up, before I come in to the crib, I'm stopping past the club for

a short time, and Tweet, can you call Tech? "Tell him to meet me at the club
so we can talk"

"Baby, I can just tell him, he's in the other room."

"Other room, tell that niggah to get the fuck out of my house?"

"Baby, he's not inside your house"

"Wait, where are you now Tweet?"

"I'm at the spot"

"At the spot, Bitch, what the fuck are you doing at the spot?"

"Baby, I'

"Baby I, my ass! Get your ass out the spot now!"

"But baby"

"Bye Tweet."

He hung up. I looked at Kim and said

"I got uh go! But think you for the heads up on Tech."

My hand rested on the doorknob as I said my last words. Inside the other
room Tech and Vick are dressed Tech redid his zipper while asking,

"How you like it baby?"

Vicky with a very unsatisfied look walked over to sit down with the TV
remote before she answered.

"Don't ask and I want hurt your feelings"

The door opened Kim and I enter the room, Vicky jumped up with joy as she
said

"Ladies have I got something to tell you."

[143]

My responds to her was

"Well I got to go home so walk me to the car and tell me on the way. O' Yes, Tech, Booker T. Called and said, "Meet him at the club A.S.A.P."

As I left the spot accompanied by Kim and Vick who acted as jaunty as a young schoolchild with gossip. Her every movement was full of energy so I asked,

"Ok little lady what was so important?"

Vicky went into her true confession,

"Ladies, when the two of you went into the stockroom, me and Tech, did the damn thing"

Teasingly I asked,

"What thing did you guys do?"

With exact words she said,

"We fucked"

Kim's eyes went wild then she questioned,

"How was it?"

Vick quickly and loudly replied,

"He got a short ass dick plus the nigga can't fuck at all."

Everyone doubled over into a good hard laugh from that news. Not yet, to my car, we noticed Tech was walking behind us. Shit we laughed even harder as we all stopped—stepped—back, to look at him while he pass--by to get to his Car. We were still laughing when he pulled away from the curb.

[144]

Tech

Tech stood 5'9 head to foot with a dark chocolate skin tone. His daily appearance was that of a young thug with his jeans hanging off his ass. I've continually tried to help Tech understand that thugging was not how one looks, but the way one reacts to a situation. Suggesting he try switching up his clothing sometime just to throw people off.

"Niggah we are up scale criminals and that means we don't look like corner thugs all the time."

Into one ear and out of the other happened to most of the words of wisdom from me. Tech had a way of cutting sound off when he did not want to hear it. He came from a house full with a fighting damn near everyday. He cultivated this ability called selective hearing. His mother and her live in boyfriend had a drinking problem so strong they had beer to drink when there was no food for Tech to eat. First, he blocked the loud fights out with the loudness of TV. By age, 11 he dared to hit the department stores. Stealing clothes so he could look cool like every one else at school. Name brand jeans and shoes, he just walked into the place changed into what he wanted and walked. This action had him in the same jeans for three or 4 days but that was the in thing for younger dudes. By the age of 15, he met a 35-year-old woman with two kids at the downtown mall. He moved into her home and became an instant daddy. Now she got him on food, money for his pocket and his clothing. That was until she saw him with a sweet hot thing kissing, in the park {busted}.   Some words

[145]

passed back and forth between Tech and his provider, and then she jumped back into her car and left. The old chick went straight home and took all the shit she had got this nigga over the year and a half they were together, put all that shit on the front yard then set the shit on fire. Dumb ass Tech came home while the shit was still smoking. His plan was to kiss her ass for forgiveness. That young man knocked for two hours begging please baby let me in saying all--type of shit, to the door but she did not open up while other dudes walked pass shaking there heads and laughing at him. Then a car pulled up to the curb, and inside this car was the older woman and two other people. She lowered the car window and he seen her and she seen him, but before he could say, "*baby please*" the car took off again while the people laughed aloud. Poor Tech stood there not only looking stupid but also felt stupid too for knocking on the door all this time when she was not even home.

At 19, he hooked up with a gang of thieves. Tech and two other people would go into the department store stealing things to return with out a receipt (Retail theft.) Two of the $14.99, smoke alarms and a large box of $12.50 Tylenol, placed into a bag. Some days it was just a$21.00 Perfume. These types of things are under $50.00 so they're exchangeable with out a receipt. The money comes in slow but at the end of the day, the gang could split up three or four hundred dollars. The down side to this game was an employee would start to remember a frequent return person and give them a hard time about not having a receipt. This was what was going on the day Tech and I met at the customer care counter.

Tech had teething jell for babies; bringing it back, the clerk asked why? He responded with some stupid ass answer then starts to flirt with her. I stood looking on at this dude with the weakest game I have ever over heard. Now the clerk tells him no receipt no money. Next, the two of them are arguing and the customer service line got longer. That is when I stepped up and said,

"Please pardon my brother and his rudeness"

As I, spit the game of a true pimp on her; she gave up the money for the shit and $10.00 over, as she counted out the change, she was looking into my cool brown eyes. I handed Tech the money then I handed the woman my rain check for a 71inchTV then paid $ 1,372.00 for it. Tech and I waited at the front door. We came to know each other better talking of how great I dealt with that situation.

When the stock guy showed up with the large TV box on a flat cart the three of us walked out to my car and placed the large box into the trunk. Damn box was too big to close so I tied the top down. I reached into my pocket and removed a knot of money then handed it to the stock guy. Tech saw its size and commented,

"That was a big ass tip."

While I got into the Road Master I asked Tech if he was coming Tech got in and off we road. Back at my spot Tech helped with the large TV box while he complained,

"Damn man this fucker is heaver then shit."

"I know man set the thing down now, shit I aint fuck'n up my back."

Together we set it down and then I tore open the box exposing the contents.5

[147]

computer laptops, 2 small printers, 10 I-pods, and 5 small CD players.
"Holy shit this was on the one, man you got game and I want in"

This happen five years ago Tech and I have been eating well, and working together on a number of jobs that I set up. Tech has tried to set up some jobs but he never had the info or the timing right so his shit definitely went to the side. Although he thought, we would do it later. However, tonight it all ends. Tech should be on his way to meet me at the club. If I'm right, he should be in deep thought about pulling a take over; only one of us will walk out of the club tonight.

Tech was roll playing so hard he don't see the red light as his car blow through it. The lights came on behind him so he had to pull it over. It did not take long for the officer to pass out a ticket for running the red light. Back onto the road now, Tech was super hot. He's' talking to himself,
"Fuck Booker T. he thinks he's the boss, his club, his money, his bitches, shit he even got the coolest wife. Booker T. will not be expecting me to pull the 9mm on him and take him out. Damn aint everyday a man can find a lady to go along with a nigga pimping and be friends with the hoes. After tonight, all that shit will be mine. Fuck I got to deal with him before he finds out I didn't kill Fat and that I cut a deal with him to let him live."

As Tech heads for the club, I am patiently, awaiting his arrival. Seated at my desk checking the parking lot for Tech's bitch—ass, while doing some

[148]

rolls playing too.

"Why Yo! Why did u lie to me knowing what I would do if or when I found out?"

I got a little something for u Tech my boy. I remember the last time all us men had assembly. LiL Don's and Tech huddled up in conversation. Don and Tech together, oh—Shit, Now it's starting to come together. First, it was Kid, then Tiny then J now my ass, ok. Damn! Why dudes want to start crossin? Are they trying to take over or are these two muthafuckers the police. My shit is straight I aint going to jail."

Tech pulled into the parking lot parked in front of the club door. He paused inside his old school pimped out Cutlass to check his gun for bullets and to make sure to have the safety fixed. His final movement before getting out was to place his gun into the small of his back thinking he can do a quick pull. Tech used his key to let himself into the club. A large warehouse cut up into three rooms, one for R&B, and one for Jazz that opened only on weekends. Then there is the striper side that opened every night. The office was located on the second floor,

Tech walked through the club and on up the steps to the office door that set open. I'm seated at my desk looking up at Tech when he entered the room.

"Hey Tech," flowed from my mouth.

"Sup Booker T., you wanted me?"

"Yeah, man, I just needed to know how much Fats offered you to let him live?"

[149]

Tech still standing now with his hands on his waist, heart pumped loud as hell. *"What the fuck you talking about man I killed Fats"*

My eyes still on Tech I shock my hard to say,

"No Tech, I killed Fats before I killed that pink ass fountain. See when I went back into the house I heard something moving up stairs, so I went to check it out, and there he was Fat daddy trying to stand up still weak from the ass kicking I put on him. So now Tech; tell--me what type of deal, did you cut with Fats?"

With balls of steel Tech pulls his 9mm on me while laughing about getting the up on me. Then he got the crazy man look in his eyes while saying,

"Niggah I have eaten your leftovers for the last time. Now—Tech—gone—be—the--boss, you got me Mr. Booker T.?"

I just looked at this ungrateful ass niggah and then I asked again

"Tech tell me, how much was the deal with Fats"

The words that boldly came out Tech's mouth before the bang, bang sound echoed through the air were. *"Half of his set up niggah what?"* Tech dropped down to his knees then on down onto his face.

The whole time while seated there at my desk, I held my 9mm pointed up at Tech's body. The bullet hit his chest traveled up out the back of his head. With Tech dead on the floor,

I jumped into action to stop this niggah from bleeding all over the place. Anticipating what went down, would go-down tonight, I had some things to help keep my club clean. The use of some rubber gloves, calking or putty and a large plate of gangster lucky, all of this shit greatly needed to pull this plan together.

First, I quickly put on a pair of rubber gloves, and then I picked up, opened the calking/putty, and started packing the bullet holes. When I was sure, it would hold I asked my good friend Tech,

"Well niggah!-u-think this shit gona hold? What you say? It should work for a short time, good I thought so too."

Now I can use the gangster luck to remove the body, because traveling to dispose of Tech's dead body many things could go wrong.

With one quick snatch up off the floor, I had one of Tech's arms over my shoulder and my hand on the back of his jeans while Tech's feet dragged the floor as I walked. When I approached the exit door, I could see this greedy fucker never locked the door behind himself. I'm thinking I can kick the door open without having to put the body down. I raised my foot to kick when the door opens up.

"Hey, Booker T. you closed up yet? Oh shit, let me help you. It looks like your boy out cold let me get the car door"

With a smile, I just kept it pushing no thank you dude or nothing. After I had Tech inside his Cutlass, I walked back to lock the club door. As I did so, this drunken dude acted surprised, while I put the key into the lock of the door.

"Damn man u closed my bad, ok I'm out, see you some other day"

As if, he could get a drink for the doors. I kept the flow with what I had to do.

With Tech in the passenger seat of his own car, I got into the drivers seat and started up the car. Destination: the railroad tracks. There was an express train every night at 3:17AM and its 2:57AM now I have to move my ass to get there on time. With the car in root I'm thinking

"There won't be much left after the express train, but that's ok with me."

Once Tech's car sat on the railroad track, I walked away and never looked back.

As I walked down Lockbourne over to Wilson Ave, I heard the impact of the car and train but I could not hear the rescue squad, police and fire trucks going to the wreck.hat night I climbed into bed and pulled myself close to Tweet, holding her so tight It woke her up to ask

"Baby what's wrong, what?" For a time I said nil just held her close. Then sympathetically I spoke, *"Tech gone baby, he gone."*

My wife Tweet had no questions for her husband as the words *"he--gone"* said it all. That night our bodies held on to each other all the way through our sleep, in the morning I opened up her nightshirt and helped myself to her nipples. She slowly opened her eyes to the feeling of both breast worked on at the same time. A the types of things that will drive her crazy; her right hand went up to grabbing hold of some of the hair on my head, further encouraging me to go on. Knowing she's' ready I raises myself on top placing that big thing into her wet pot. I used just the head first in and out adding a little more meat with each hump to amplify the joy, within her. When I feel her at that doorway of shouting out my name, I shoot hard to the bottom. Yes, that's it, now the neighbors know daddies home and handling the biz. After letting her enjoy herself for a time, I whisper into her ear *"baby I need you to catch this*

[152]

one" Tweet nods her head yes as she can feel me going for the end. I worked it so we both could enjoy that good shit as I moved fast then slow. Now it was time for me to shoot. She could tell this by my breathing as it changed to me blowing through my teeth, and then I pushed back rising on my knees leaning back. She raise foreword and place her mouth over my throbbing meat drinking that entire force I had inside me, while she did so I breathed out slowly the air I held inside alone with the words "*I Love you baby.*"

We laid there for a time in each other's arms before I looked over; it was nine o'clock, so I put on the TV flipping through the channels for the news. The big story of the morning was, "A drunk driver and the 3:17 Express Train collided" The News Caster quoted "Last night a car driven onto the tracks collided with the 3:17 train. The drivers name unknown." The police representative stated on the News,

"Due to the damage caused by the train, we are hoping to use dental records to identify the driver."

"Booker T. with out Tech!" At this moment, my head won't leave my head alone. "Man shit all fucked up inside of me, my dog gone and I am the one that had to put him down."

As I hear Tweet was moving around the house, I tried to make sense of this whole thing that went on last night. Then it hit me! "If a man's dog gets sick with rabies he has to put it down, it may hurt but it has to happen. That's what happened to Tech's ass; he got sick so I put him down. Ok, I can live with that." The house phone sounded off loud enough to cut into my thoughts, and

[153]

then Tweet shouted,

"It's for you baby, it's LiL Don on the phone."

I said, *"Hello"* with a hesitant voice.

"Hey niggah, what you got up on your end 4 to day?'

Lil Don talking to me as if all was well; I'm still not feeling him so I said,

"Shit"

"Well if it aint too much shit do you think we can hang some?"

"What you got planned" I asked.

"Shit, when you think you coming this way?" Lil Don asked.

"In a short bit, first I got to go to the club for something then I'll be over"

"OK"

"Cool see you them."

LiL Don's bank Scam

In the Road Master on my way over to LiL Don's crib, I'm still fucked up inside about Tech crossing me. If only there was someone, I could talk to about this whole thing. It would be nice to process, back and forth to find an answer for why Tech felt the way he did against me. I treated Tech like a brother and if he worked harder, I would have given him a fifty--fifty split on everything. Damn, why it has to be so hard to find a true road dog, that ride—a--die partner? I'm down--right tired of all the fast life, the hoes, club, dope and all the bullshit that goes with it. If only my boo Tweet and I could go off somewhere just the two of us to live. Bright red light brought my car and me to a full stop. A black Volkswagen car pulled up beside me with some hot ass chick. She was giving me the eyes as I give her a courteous smile. "I'm so, so tired of this shit too" then in a low voice I said to her "Bitch you can't even afford me with your Volkswagen driven ass" grateful for the light change I continued on my way to LiL Don's crib. Thoughts of the night LiL Don asked to buy into the club tap into my brain.

"Be partner/ half owner having some say so about what goes on in this club was that what you're asking? I asked while laughing in LiL Don's face. No way niggah but if have I ever decided to sell, you will be the first to know."

I have always envisioned my son Turtle and I running this club together whenever Turtle got his head right. Now Turtle locked up, Tech dead and I

[155]

know I could be on the way up state, I can't hold on to it with out stress from
up State. I'll ask Don if he still interested in being an owner of a club."

I pulled up to a bunch of young dudes cluttered around LiL Don's porch. I
got out and walked up nodding and saying, "sup" as LiL Don introduced
Booker T. A.K.A. Suspect to all these young bucks standing and setting from
the steps to the porch rail. Then I asked,

"So what u got up for the day man?"

"Just shooting some pool, maybe get something to eat; it has been a minute
since we hung out."

However, LiL Don never moved after his comment.

"Ok Don so when we gone take off and who all will ride in your car?"
Showing my impassions; which was a good thing because it got the nigga
moving as he said,

"There you go starting shit niggah! First off all these guys got somewhere to
go and it aint with us." With LiL Don standing up and making that statement
all the dudes started walking off while saying *"later Don, nice meeting you*
Booker T."

"Second, we are up in your shit today! So let's go." We both got into my
Road Master and began the ride out Main Street to the 12-ball poolroom. As
the car rolled down the road, a conversation started with LiL Don questioning
me about Tech. *"So when's the last time you talked to your bro Tech?"*
That was question number one,

"It's been one or two days"

[156]

"That the norm for him to just dip out and not get back to you?"

OK, number 2

"Not really but why?"

"Well the word is that your bro Tech drove his car into the late night train the other day. The police know it was his car but can't prove it was his body because the niggah never did go to the Dentist or the Doctors so there aint no records to math the dude from the train wreck."

My come back at that was,

"Shit the News I got on TV never did say what type of car it was and no it aint strange for Tech to disappear for one or two weeks for some good--ass pussy, he done dug up into." Silence enters the car thick enough to cut with a knife then I questions. *'Damn do—u--really think Tech done drove his shit on the tracks?"*

*"*Naw, *but I do think someone did it for him. You like a brotha to him aint you? Did he tell you he was beef-in with someone?"* Questioned LiL Don

"Fuck no or I would have handled it along side da niggah!"

"I would think so," taunted LiL Don in a mocking way before saying.

"Ok then Tech should call you soon, if not the report I got of his car was true and your bro Tech has gone onto some other place." The rest of our time spent together went pass without talk of Tech. However, LiL Don did have some money business to talk over at dinner.

"Check this shit out Book I got a call from my man up in Detroit talking about him and his boys on the road for here. Dee's fuckers are big timers' I'm talking killers and they need help to transfer funds through the banks. Dee's

*man is paying eight hundred to every one that joins in on this thing. So is u in
or not?"*

Hum!

"Eight hundred, shit you know I'm in, so what's the buzz about." LiL Don
goes on telling me

*"Last year around this time dude tried driving through and lost a quarter of a
mill to the police. Therefore, this time they want a number of people with bank
accounts to let them wire a deposit of 2,300.00 in cash into an account. Come
the next day you take out the money hand over 1500. Then you keep the rest
for the work you did. The question now, how many folk you know will do this
thing with out getting stupid about the money because I'm telling u man these
dudes are killers about there shit. As for me I got my wife and my too broads
getting in on this, right there I got me 2,400.00 Out the door on that end but I
need two hundred from everyone I put in on this that gives you six for doing
nothing but going to the bank."*

*"Damn that do sound good but I have to talk to Tweet because she was the
one with the bank account but she'll do it if I say so. Count me in but tell me
when this thing gone jump off?"*

*"I think this week but I'm on hold until I get the word so when I know
something you will know it too."*

"Cool hit me up on that shit."

The pair of us stood at the check out when I asked,

*"Hey have you heard any thing on Kid or Tiny lately how they doing?" "Not
nothing on them I did call Kids wife and she got real nasty with me so I aint*

[158]

calling no more and Tiny! Fuck that niggah, hope he don't never try to get in touch with me." My only response to all that shit. *"Damn ok, I think it's time to call it a night for me."*

Very little was talked about on the way back to LiL Dons crib as he exited the Road Master, he said to me.

"Talk to you later on the money thing."

I answered *"Cool, get with you then."* I never did talk to Tweet about the money wire until the day I got the call from LiL Don to bring her to his crib to talk to a dude that works for some bank for which the name of the bank never got disclosed to Tweet or me.

"What's your full name on your bank account, and what bank you work with? What's the account number and how long having you banked there?"

Tweet answered each question with only one question for the interviewer.

"Now we are talking a cash wire transfer into my account right?"

"Yes! It will go in on the twenty eighth posts on the twenty ninth for you to take it out."

"Ok", she said in a soft voice.

I ended the meeting with the words

"Ok, we are out of here" as I stood up and extended a hand to help Tweet to her feet.

On the way home Tweet questioned if, LiL Don had his wife in on this shit. All I could do was tell her what he told me.

"He said he used her and two of his broads why you asking baby?"

"Because, we fuckin with LiL Don baby any shit going on with him, aint never right for no-one but him."

I felt what my wife was saying, but I have full trust in my man Lil Don. I had to tell my wife,

"U right Tweet but he aint never burned me. Its all-good baby trust me if you don't trust him ok."

Thursday the 29th the wire went into her bank just as predicted Fri morning 30th I accompanied my wife to take out the 2,800 every thing went right all the way down to me handing LiL Don all but 600.00 of the money. Tweet questioned me as we road down the street coming back from the bank.

"Why u have to give the money to LiL Don?"

I answered,

"LiL Don was to hold all money until the dudes get there from collecting other places." Ok, Tweets part now done I took her back home then I went to get a number of other women I put in on to this thing. My pockets were fatter at the end of the day. Sitting around LiL Dons crib where a number if men picking with the young pimp joking how my stuff was on the one for getting that money every thing was great.

The next day was the first of the mouth I went out and bought me an old school Lincoln I've had my eye on for some time. Tweet had direct deposit on her Crazy check, child support, and paycheck so she went to the ATM machine for some money. Where she found out It was over drown by some 28 00.00

Damn her money was sucked up by the bank leaving it over drown. The whole thing was a bank swindle and I was in the middle of it. It was a counterfeit check made out to tweet and deposit into her bank account. Tweet went to LiL Don demanding her money back before calling me

"Yes, I went to see that piece of shit about mine!" and he told me.   *"I aint got it Tweet I gave it to them men" "Ok, then u saying I had a 2800.00 lick put on me thanks to you and you got 2or 3 hundred off the top so give me that part back"*

"Hell no! Shit Booker T. got 6 hundred off it too, go get that back, because I aint got nothing to give back"

I just started to laugh I squinted my eyes and slowly shook her head in disbelief. Inside my mind a voice shouted,

"Killem –do this fuck,"

Feelings of rage turned my face to a cold stare before I said in a soft tone voice

"In all my years in the game I have never had a lick put on me. U got this one right now but it aint over bitch."

"Are you threatening me Tweet? I don't like that shit Man don't make threats."

"Fuck u and what--ever you don't like, I'm telling u Don, and this shit here aint over until I sit on top."

LiL Don knew of the stories of me, as a killer putting muthafucka into the hospital, so now he knew he has to watch his back. I got up to go for the door when LiL Don said,

"hay, Tweet look I know this thing fucked u all up money wise so how bout I give u a ounce of green on front and you bring me a yard back on it"

"Ok, so now you gone put me to work for you right? The way I see it you owe me so you should just give me some of them things with no pay back on it and if it aint that way you can kiss my ass then again with all the money my husband getting u think we hurting for cash muthafucka? Just what's your problem man? Damn can you not see, it's about the fuckin lick, bitch? That's why I am here in your face. Ok, tell u what, take the money and the green you got for me to sell and shove all that Shit up into your wife's pussy."

With that, LiL Don tightened up as if he might hit me but I never flinched, because deep down inside I wished the bitch ass nigga would hit me then I would have grounds to kill him out right. With no more words out of his door I walked to my car, I had one leg into my green convertible when Booker T. drove up the street super fast and started parking the Road Master. Fully seated inside the car I started it up allowing it to run until my husband stood at the side of the door. He looked into my eyes as he said, *"um sorry"* then he bent down and kissed me before stepping back to let me pull off. I never did tell him about the bank fuck up I did not have to because everyone else had.

Mad as hell I walked up to LiL Don's door and knocked harshly on it. Quickly it opened with a protest of the racket

"Dude u aint got to knock on my door like that man."

With out the offer of an apology I entered and took a seat

"Man I need to hear something about the lick that got put on my wife and other girls." ""What would u have me say other then the men came got that money and took off."

"Don Man I put my word on that shit for every one to be all fucked up on my word that came from your word." Now very up set I asked one more question, *"So what did your wife say about this thing?"*

"Man I never put my wife in on shit. My wife or my broads' aint part of this shit"

"Hold the fuck up u means I got my peoples in on this on u saying u had your peeps in on this shit and you played me man."

At that moment, I felt sick to my stomach with building fury, betrayal and deception of another man thought to be a best friend. A spiritual father through my recovery process has just shit on me. Damn! I believed this man when I couldn't believe shit that was going on inside my own head. The pain

[163]

of betrayal from Tech and now LiL Don, I knew I should have backed up from this nigga. Now to be fleece by him, fuck tears fluttered in my eyes while feeling and thoughts of doing this man right here right now.

I'm truly hurt and full of thoughts of knocking him the fuck out, but bitch ass men like him always calls the police. I just got up and walked out the crib there really was nothing for the two of us to discuss. LiL Don knew better then to make his punk ass offer to sell some green on a front to me. As I road down the street my cell phone buzzed

"Hello" came from my mouth before my ear filled with Lil Don's voice.

"Booker T., man I need to say I'm sorry about this hole thing man, I did not know shit was gone go down like it did. I did lie about my wife being in on the thing because I knew if I said that you would get into it also. However, I never include my wife in on business and that's code for me. I'll cop to the wife lie but that other shit came as a surprise to me too." Real stuff, there was nothing Lil Don could do to undo all he had done. So I said,

"Its cool man I'll get back later"

Then I hung up. No bullshit from LiL Don helped the way I felt or how I will look at LiL Don from here on out. All the trust between us was gone. From here on everything out of LiL Don's mouth will be considered to be a lie and I'll give that niggah a long handle. My new code will be "never hook--up on shit else with him and spend less time with LiL Don.

Time passed, I keep it pushing with the pimpin game, and dope pushin along with caring for my club to bad Tech never did show up. One or two months later LiL Don called me with some miniature talk. A week later LiL Don called asking me to come to church and support him. Enjoy some good food after he finishes playing the drums. Being a friend, I went. After church plans for the two of us to get together tomorrow about 5 pm and shoot some pool up at the hall on Main Street.

I got to LiL Don's crib at 4pm and sat around on the porch talking shit with Paul LiL Don's nephew. Don called his nephew into the crib for a moment then Paul stepped back out and asked me,

"Please shoot me up north right quick?"

Not thinking I said,

"Come on niggah!"

I got some time so the two of us jump into the Road Master. Paul has a book bag on his shoulder and tosses' it on the back seat. I travailed seven blocks down LiL Don's street when the police pull me over. It's Bat—man again, the same cop that took Kid down town and he has both us out of the Road Master. The big question here for me was, why am I being pulled over. I turned no corners, ran no stop signs, and with daylight, they can't say he got a light out, O-yes and the sounds were not on. Long story short I had 3 ounces green up under my seat, but when the book bag was took out the back and asked whose bag? We both held a closed mouth so every one went to jail. I was not thinking about the owner of the car will own the bag. Paul and I get out on future indictments. Inside that book bag was a 9mm fully loaded with hollow points and 32 grams of hard and once again, I'm up set with self for fucking with bitch ass LiL Don.

[165]

Ask yourself this question
"What is unconditional love to me?

Then look at your answer, is it acceptable to all!

An Apple off the Tree

I have a son and two daughters that my husband accepts as his own. Everyone calls my son Turtle! Not because he's slow in movement, on the contrary it's because the little dude is known to go hard. As a kid, all he had was two sisters and me, a crack head mom. His older sister Sherry had long gone from the nest and had a family of her own. My younger daughter and Turtle, left with me as a mother and I did all I could so they would never know I was on crack. Their father never wanted kids so the niggah never spent time with his son or daughter. Too bad, that is his loss.

It was normal for the dope boys to be around my crib running in and out. Thinking back it was cool how they made the sale, and then pass little Turtle some cash on the down low while headed back out the door. There was days when my high came down and I seen Turtle and his little sister eating candy. My question was,

"Where u find candy money at boy?"

Turtle would say,

"Your friend gave me five or ten when he was here earlier today mom."

Other ways Turtle made money was to walk pit bulls everyday or run to the store for a blunt shell. Some days while I was in my own world getting high, he sat around at their crib and played with their guns learning how to load and unload them. The dope boys also showed him how to bundle up the twenty sacks while they talked the game talk. Seeing boys not much older then him flipping everyday and getting all that money helped Turtle to build his hunger for the game.

Thank God, getting high got old after a time for me and I got clean off the dope! This changed things around the house. The dope boys finally stop coming in and out of my crib, but they still hung out on the street corners and Turtle did too. I tried to keep my baby away from the lifestyle but he seen the money and he wanted some of it right now. Fuck later after he goes to school or has a job. His first hustle was bicycle parts to the hood for a fair price. Things went well for Turtle, until the police showed up at my house accompanied by a crying little white kid and his daddy. The white kid said some black kid punched him in the face and took his bicycle. That particular bicycle was not here at my house yet, however I knew in all probability it was on its way. The officer asked me if I knew how Turtle got all the frames and parts; he had down in the basement. I could not tell them a thing because I honestly did not know. Whenever Turtle came home with something I knew he couldn't have purchased on his own I would ask him,

"*Baby, where did you get this?*"

He would always answer,

"*I found it mommy.*"

The last thing Turtle came home giving me that "I found It mom" stuff I received a new up right washer and dryer.

My washer stopped working one day. I was cussing and talking about how sick and tired of going to the laundry I was and in the door, my son came with the very thing I needed. Did I say?

"Take it back"

Hell no I did not! Shit I hooked that fucker up and cleaned all our dirty clothes.

One other thing that may have contributed to Turtle getting into the lifestyle was the stories he heard while attending family Sunday dinners. Being clean, now my kids and I could join in on dinner at grand mamma's house. After pigging out on a lot of good soul food, everyone sat and talked about each other. The younger kids got a big kick from hearing how the older people made it through a fucked up start in life. As a child coming up how far we walked to get to school and shit like that. Changing stories from mayo sandwiches and ketchup soup, to the ass whippings, we all got from grand mamma. However, the best stories came from them talking about my life before the crack. How I killed a man and never served a day in prison. In addition, the different types of drugs I sold and never been caught. How if one of my workers hit jail and had to set over night, I come in the morning to see to them gettin free. My always having fine ass cars, my pimping two men from the same house, having them bringing me that money from then working the same job. I lived a life of a player with the three of us sleeping together. Shit, every one respected me for my game. I'm ok that it's the past for me now; I'm content sitting at the crib, while my husband was out get'n that money. Some days I would be cooking or just looking at TV, when Turtle

[169]

would throw out a question or two about life inside the game. Mom

"How come the police never ever ran up in our crib?"

A big smile grew on my face from that question, and then I softly said,

"Boy, never shit where you lay your head."

Another time he questioned me,

"Mom, what if I got to drop a niggah because of my money?"

I held a straight face while answering that question because; talk of killing a person aint no joke.

"Some times it's not about the money baby boy. Sometimes it's about respect! If you aint got that, you aint got shit! Now if it comes down to you being about your word, and you told that muthafucka what was gone happen if he didn't have your money; then drop him. Drop that muthafucka dead and then become the traveling man."

These are some of the things Turtle and I talked about as Turtle got on up into his upper teenage years and felt like he could fill my shoes.

Turtle age17 stood five nine with soft light brown skin that every young girl around the block longed to have a chance to touch. His body held the shape of a basketball player, with sexy six-pack abs and a nice firm butt. Having peach fuzz over his lip showed all the girls that he a man.

Turtle tried his hand, as a player with the girls. Five young girls calling and stopping through his crib at will, not a health thing. I saw where this was headed having done the same thing back in my player years. I knew fully what can happen when a niggah don't have some type of control on his girls. I wanted to tell my son

"Baby boy never let but one chick comes to your crib to see you and let that be the one your feel-in strong feelings for. As for the other girls, you get your ass up and go visit them at their cribs. Tell them whatever; but never, ever, let them come to your shit whenever they want to."

Play rule 101 best learned from having your own fuck ups happen. That's how I felt about it so I just sat back and watched for the fight to happen.

Turtle with his main girl lying on the sofa, chilled with a cool breeze coming in on them from the open front door. When girl number three stopped by and walked right in through the open front door.

"What the fuck man!"

Shot from her mouth, as if she had just come home from work and found Turtle fucking inside her own bed. The fight was on now with shouting and

[171]

name-calling between the two girls. Everyone went out front of the crib that stopped a fight from happening inside of my house. Things were truly heating up when a car pulled up with girl number four in it. She gets out of the car to see what the fuck was going on in front of her man's house! Only to find out she too felt played by this muthafucka named Turtle. I stood back for a time looking at this wild ass shit. Then I took my son's number one girl off to the side and asked her some questions?

"Honey do you love my son?"

"Yes ma'am"

"Do you want to be the winner here today"?

"Yes ma'am"

"Then do this, take a slow walk to the corner store and buy your man a cold pop and some potato chips. Take your time so whenever you get back here, all this bullshit will be done and over. One more thing and this maybe the hardest, but it's the most important part of the plan. Please! Don't ask him about this shit here! Just go back to you and him enjoying the rest of the day. Now do you think you can do this or not?"

"Yes ma'am, but I aint got no money."

I passed the young girl five dollars while uttering to her,

"Here take this five for cleaning my kitchen."

The young girl looked puzzled as she stated,

"I haven't cleaned your kitchen miss Tweet"

I started to laugh aloud as I leaned close to the girl's ear and said,

"I know, but you will, one day soon."

The young girl smiled softly then departed for the store. It did not take long before the police stopped by and broke the bullshit up. Turtle left sitting on the steps along with his head down looking sad as hell. His main girl was gone. His heart felt fucked up. What could he tell her to get her back? *What lie can I use*? Different things bounced through his head before the grape pop slowly came up into his face. Quickly he looked up to see his girl there with his favorite pop and some potato chips. He wanted to jump up and hug her, but he had to stay cool with his shit, he can't let her see she got a niggah on lock. While taking the stuff out of her hands he said,

"Thank you baby this is just what I needed."

The two of them sat on the front steps for a short time as he enjoyed his refreshments. He offered her some, but she said,

"No, I ate mine while I walked from the store."

As he finished his snack, he thought then to ask,

"Where you got some money from?"

She smiled while thinking about saying, *"I cleaned your mother's kitchen"* but that would be a lie so she just said,

"I got it from your mom."

It was at that point in time he knew it was I, which saved his butt once again. Money was on Turtles mind when he wasn't thanking about food or pussy. The code of getting quick money in the hood is

Whenever you see a sucker slipping, get him! It does not matter **where** the

[173]

fuck you are at, pull that shit out on him! Muthafucka, know **how** to use it to get paid. Those words right there are what Turtle learned to live by on the streets of Columbus Ohio. He may have been the youngest in the pack of dudes he hung with, but he had the biggest set of balls. That made him the head niggah in charge. See listening to the stories of how I got down back in my day, and he's hearing how his step dad Booker T. was putting it down now up in the short north of the CO. He had to go even harder, stepping over into the big boys' money game. His boys often questioned why his step dad would not put him on his team. His basic answer to that shit was,

"Muthafucka don't question me", while looking crazy like he a killer.

However, the real story was that Booker T. couldn't take the chance of his only son being fucked up on these streets behind some of his dope. Then to the best way to get this game deep down into your soul, was to get it on your own.

Turtle's first night out on the prowl for that big boy money was by himself. He could not take the chance of his boys seeing him look scared when it came time to bust that thing. He had spent a lot of time playing with his gun up in his room. He stood in the marrow looked at himself as he pulled it out quick like a cowboy. He even shot it one or two times up in the air. Nevertheless, could he shoot a man? Damn! If he bitches-out no one could every no that shit.

He had to go it all alone; when he sat back in the cut on Livingston, it was a cold ass Thursday night in Dec. A Gold Cadillac with floating rims doing laps around the block had turtle stuck with thoughts of the pay off. Inside the

Cadillac, he saw a fat-ass big ballen niggah. Turtle figured dude must have been looking to get his dick sucked by the right hoe. This sucker had his window down showing off a big ass platinum chain on his nick. Turtles whispered the words,

"This niggah looked like his pockets are fat as hell and waiting for me."

Turtle faded up into the cut of a doorway by the red light. The next time the Cadillac stopped for that red light, Turtle quickly moved up to the side of the driver's door. The driver looked up and said.

"What can I do for you young blood"

Turtle has flashed his 9mm while he held a smile and responded,

"U, feel like feed-den me OG?" 9mm revealed to the man.

The OG started to laugh as he said,

"U, got to be joking with me"

That was when Turtle shot him in the leg while asking

"Is it still funny OG"

With on more laugher the OG peeled all his shit out of all his pockets. Turtle tapped the 9mm to the big chain reminding him to take it off his nick. The two diamond filled rings, and a bird of hard out of the glove compartment made Turtle smile even harder. With everything passed out of the window, Turtle laughed aloud while saying,

"Now I think you should go straight to the nearest hospital OG."

The OG just set there as if he was in shock or in disbelief, that he was just got stuck up. Turtle used a more powerful tone without laughter when he said,

"OG, Dude! I think you should go to the hospital now before I shoot you

again."

The gold Cadillac did zero to 50 in seconds up the street. The take on that one lick was big, so big Turtle couldn't wait to do it again. This time he would take his boys

It was not cold even thou it was a winter day and he had business on High street .Over on the short north end of High. As he walked toward Town St, he came to a costume shop. There in the window was a mannequin wearing a cop suit. Without a second thought, he went into the store to see what types of other costume they had and how much it would cost to rent one. The clerk turned out to be a young college student that likes to blow the sticky green. Turtle just happen to have some Sticky-icky on him. The two guys stepped outside to puff, puff and pass the blunt. As they talked about the rental of an "S.W.A.T" costume, that is four costume to be precise. The clerk quoted,

"For a quarter of this shit you can get them all for a weekend on me. Pick them up on Friday and return them on Monday."

"Cool, do I need ID to get them?"

"Fuck no man we cool, I know who you are."

With that, the two young-men busted out with a good weed laugh. Turtle left that shop with one thought.

"Who will be the mark?"

It took him two days but he came up with a spot. A trap house at the bottom of Wilson Ave, dope fiends keep it pop-in. Money has to be good up in there. The plan was to hit this crib as S.W.A.T. would. Put everyone on the floor,

[176]

snatch and grab whatever there was and get out nobody gets hurt. Friday five o'clock just before closing Turtle picked up the "S.W.A.T" costumes in exchange for the sticky-icky green. Next, he got all the key players of this game to his crib,

(The names where changed to protect them).

The costume package consisted of four S.W.A.T shirts and masks everyone will dress in all black from the feet up just like S.W.A.T. We had $tink-boy Turtles best friend, $tink-boy's little brother was the driver and one more niggah, name Jo-Jo and of course Turtle. They all got dressed $tink-boy got his 9mm, Jo-Jo got his short shotgun and Turtle got his 9mm and they looked just like the real thing. In the car, Turtle went over the order of operations. Wilson Ave they all jump out of the car, moving slow and quiet crouched down like the police do. but they aint got no battering ram to bust in the door. So there forced to stand on the side of the crib and wait for someone to come in or out to allow the rush in to rob this place. This is a main street so cars are passing by looking at S.W.A.T. written big as day on the back of all their shirts plus the guns and masks; no one dare fuck with them.

At last, two dope fiends came out of the door having words with each other. Hey, opportunity knocked so every one jumped to answer the door. Turtle shouts as he moves in first!

"*S.W.A.T get down!*"

The bitch at the door tries to close it, but Turtle kicks it back hard!

"Boom"

[177]

Knocking her back up against the wall, as the door blew open. Again, he shouts for the second time,

"*S.W.A.T every one down on the floor now*"

$tink-boy and the others shoved the two crack fiends back into the crib. There was seven crack heads down on the floor and two dealers. Turtle gets one of the dealers up to his feet and takes him off into the other room. As the leader he has to do more then the rest of his scared ass team. Standing in the other room, he asked dude

"*Where is it?*"

This dude just stands there, like he's hard or he thinks it's a game. Turtle hits this bitch ass niggah hard as hell up side the face.

"*Wop*"

"*Where is it at Niggah?*"

The dude grabbed his head with one hand and used the other to happily point to where the money and some jewelry were. Turtle was the only one of his crew in the room so this safe was a personal com-up. However, he knew some dope had to be here, so one more time,

"*Where is it at?*"

He shouted but dude did not talk quick enough so he hits him again in the head.

"*Wop*"

The gun go's off this time. Damn! That bitch ass niggah got so scared he passed the fuck--out on the floor,

"*Boom*"

[178]

Fear shook Turtle for a hot second, thinking he had killed dude, but there was no blood poring out onto the floor. Turtle took a second to thank the gangster gods for their help on this one. Then he calls to $tink-boy in the other room

"Bring that other niggah in here to me!"

With out a second call his orders where carried out. This dude stepped into the room his eyes bugged out as he looked down at his friend on the floor. Dude started crying and begging for his life right off the rip.

"Please man! Don't kill me! I'll do what ever, just don't kill me." Turtle tried hard not to laugh at what this punk ass niggah was crying about it took a second but turtle finally told him,

"Just tell me where the dope is and we'll let you live"

Dude had no problem giving everything up.

The team departed with 10 pound's of good green and 71oz of hard. In the ride, everyone had a good laugh talking about dude begging for his life. In addition, how they all thought Turtle had killed the first niggah in the room. Back at the crib, they all split up the green and the hard from the hit. $tink-boy brother stood to leave with his take on the deal and said,

"Yo Turtle man, I thought you killed that dude fore real man. Look if you got some other shit you doing, leave me out, I'm cool, you muthafuckers are too hard for me."

"Ok, niggah no probe, just remember, to keep your mouth closed and you won't find out just how hard I am."

Turtle spoke his words while looking at $tink-boy, because he's the one that brought this weak ass niggah to a gunfight without a gun.

[179]

Second chance to ask yourself this question
"What is unconditional love?

Then look at your answer, is that what you're giving!

Part 3

Journal entry 4

Week three and a half of watching this short piece of shit; "Man how I hate this fucker with a passion. Soon his family will be putting together some slow songs to sing. To bad, not all the flowers in the world will change the smell of him being the rat that he is. Booker T., kid, Turtle and Tiny would be free on the streets had he not sold them out to the police to save his own ass. Damn I keep thinking about it, but I just cannot see how I will do this bitch ass niggah! Shit the police kept my 38, after I did me a niggah in Pittsburgh. So how can I get up close to kill this fucker with out getting blood all over me, I got to walk away free one more time? Ok let me look closely at this thing

One: The kill should be up close or maybe not.

Two: can't have blood all over me.

Three: I must be in, out quick. Damn If I could use a knife. No! Because he is a man and me being a female I may not win the struggle with him. Now, if I can get him while he is still setting down inside his car, maybe? This calls for even more research.

Turtle Took It on the Road

Everyone in the hood talked about a gang of dudes that would come into a crib to get all you got. Don't matter if you home or not these fuckers hit quick and hard, so be on your guard. The stories told by the dudes not to embarrassed, to tell what happen to them said,

"Man one minute I was chilling, and the next minute, I was down on the floor praying they don't kill me."

Yes, my son Turtle, and his boys had did a number on Columbus Ohio. Sticking up dudes, on and off the block had everyone in fear of where they will hit next. If you had it and they know of it, kiss it all good byes. They became known to take all your shit plus splitten your skull if you take to long passing it off. Once the face got a name "Turtle" some threats started to come, but because of his dad Booker T, being one of the lords of one of the biggest gangs straight out of Baltimore, City a muthafucka thought twice about fuckin with that dude. Some of the big wigs got together and came to Booker T. respectfully, like, you know, asking if he will please do something with his son Turtle.

Therefore, he did just that at the next Sunday dinner. Booker T. took his son out in the back yard where the two of them could talk, not as father and son but as two hard-core men. I saw the two of them from the kitchen window. My need to know kicked in and I quickly put together two glasses of cool-aid with ice and took it out to them as I sat in the open seat and passed them out I listened.

[183]

"Dude you got to know how hurt your mother would be, if and when someone puts one of them things up into you."

Turtle slowly nodded his head as his eyes moved to meet mine.

"The road you riding leads straight to the grave and you have to do shit a different way before that happens. Tell me how you set with work and cash?"

Turtle sat shoulders humped over with his head hung low; he knew this shit was coming but not this soon.

"My boys and I are setting pretty good"

"What the fuck you call pretty good?" Booker T. asked with a little deeper tone. Hearing the aggression come in his father's voice Turtle set up straight and said

"I and my boy got 2 stacks a piece in pocket, but I got 50 stacks put up in a box for hard times. Then we got 3 whole bird and 1 and half pounds of good green."

Booker T. had a prideful look when he said to Turtle.

"Damn boy you have been gettin it. Well this is what you bout to do. All that robbing is over; I'm talking all done! Now it's time to go to work, sell that shit to get your money and not here in Columbus. This place here, dead, for you dude. You done cut to many throats here in this town you have to take Yo shit on the road. You understand what the fuck I'm telling you?"

Our son Turtle nodded his head then got up out his chair and went back into the crib. The next day Turtle got up with his partner Sticky-boy and the first word out of Sticky-boys mouth as he happily dropped down on his sofa and pulled out a blunt.

"So what you got up foe today my niggah? Is we gone get money or what?"
Turtle sounded sickly when he said,

*"Shit, my dad and I had that talk yesterday man. All that rob-n Niggah's for
their shit is over for me. Nevertheless, it gets worse dude, my dad said he
thinks I should get out of town for a minute. Take my game on the road to
push the dope I got. So I thought on it and it came to me about dude that used
to get money with us, damn what the fuck is his name? O k, I got it his name
was Drake he said, there is some good and quick money down in a town
called Altoona PA. I got his number in my old phone we can call him see how
shit is flowing and hit it off down there, So you in? "*

With out a thought $tink-boy answered,

"Hell yes, when we leaving?"

Turtle said,

"We out this weekend if it is what it is"

So, $tink-boy and my son Turtle, sat back and got smoked the fuck out until
they passed the fuck out. That weekend Turtle took his act on the road. He
called me, to make sore I knew where he was going, while telling me how
nice his car was riding. They made only one stop and that was for gas and
food then on into Altoona. I know what he did after he got there because the
games don't change.   First thing needed was a dope fiend to let test the good
shit from out of town. Second thing post up in a fiends house let the business
come to them, that way the fiends name and crib got put out there as the spot
to cop. Soon Turtles shit was on and popin.   It took no time at all to sell out
of hard (crack) but the weed was moving so slowly $tink-boy and Turtle

[185]

smoked damn near all that shit themselves. What those people were really begging for was that boy (heroin) that shit moved fast in that little town. It did not take long before my son and his boy had taken over Altoona Pa with the drugs. Turtle spent so much time in Altoona his girl Donna started complaining about not seeing him. For real, she's just longing for some of that good dick. He hooked her up whenever he came back to Columbus to re-up but that was not enough for her. Things were cool for Turtle because he had a new piece of ass with him there in Altoona. Some 21years old cutie pie name Nicky, 5'7" 165lb. This took the edge off his dick when he felt like getting his meat sucked. Now Stick-boys girl was the sister to Turtle's girl Donna so these two bitches put there heads together and demanded to be able to come to Altoona when there dudes came home to re-up. The four of them could they chill down in Altoona together. Turtle came to me asking for my thoughts on him taking his girl down there.

"Ok, it may work but come clean to the Altoona girl Nicky about having a wifey and she coming down on the next run."

Now mind you Turtle knows all girls live off E-motions so if you play one for the other, the girl played will do her best to get you back.   Turtle and $tink-boy got a motel room up the street for their girls to chill in. Afterword all four went to the trap (crack house) $tink-boy and Turtle are bagging up getting ready for the rush by the dope fiends. Wifey (Donna) and her sister are rolling green up so everyone can blow. Turtle should have said, "NO, we got to get ready for work" but instead they were smoking weed out of this world. Everyone was getting high. Turtle now thinking with his other head takes wifey into the bathroom. Their Turtle was enjoying a bomb head job. $tink-boy chilled with the sister in the other room. Some music was on (Gucci Mane) when Turtle glanced out the bathroom window and saw Nicky headed down the street, the other girl. "Stop! Shit Stop. Turtle quickly moved out the bathroom and headed to the front door. Donna now anxious to know just what was going on trails behind him to the front door where Nicky was about to knock. Turtle pulls the door open while holding a cute smile on his face

"Hey Nicky, what's good with you?" came out of his mouth but for real he was thinking *"What the fuck? I told this bitch my wife was coming down and I would get with her later so what the fuck?"*

Nicky saw the other chick all up on Turtles back plays it cool as Turtle introduced his wifey and her sister. Donna tells Nicky *"Come on in and hit the blunt"* so she did. Nicky sat on the phone the whole time hardly hitting the blunt. Turtle definitely, was not on his Ps and Qs. He's not paying attention to what was going on around him. I guess you could say he was a niggah slip-in.

Feeling all good smoking and chilling .He seen Nicky leave, not out the front, but out the back, leaving it unlocked. Ok, Donnas' sister was upstairs, and Turtle, wifey and $tink-boy are smoking at the horseshoe counter in the kitchen. The drugs packed away in a can (Clean-X). Nobody would think fake bottom. Everything was cool until some dude comes in the back door, Turtle aint even thinking about having his gun in his waste belt, because of being caught off guard. Fuck, he can't pull it out, because dude got $tink-boy from the back, with a gun up to his head. He tells Turtle to get down on the floor. *"What do I do"*? Are thoughts moving fast through Turtles mind?

 "Shit I can run and shoot it out with this fucker? This is what I been waiting for all my life. Shit, I can feel it burning in my soul because my mother is a killer and her mother was a killer and her mother before her killed someone. I came from a long line

of badass bitches that did not mind killing a niggah if he was wrong! But what, my homey, my best friend, someone I love like a brother shit this niggah got a gun to his head."

Turtle got down on his face. Dude put Stinky-boy beside him and told Donna to sit –down over in the chair. Then dude ask

"Where it at"

   Turtle told dude

"All I got is some weed and 900.00 in cash"

He could tell dude was from NY. Dude hits every ones pockets but aint

[188]

nobody have shit but Turtle. While patting he finds the 9mm and used it to pops Turtle hard in the back of the head. Plus he pulls the 1500.00 chain off his neck before he left. Turtle kept his 3oz of hard, but he can't stay here with out a gun so he puts in a call to Booker T. and me his mother

"Dad man, come and get me or send me some money for gas so we can come back to Columbus. I'll tell you what happen when I get there."

Of course, being his mother Turtle had to tell me something now; if he called home for help, he must tell me the whole story.

Being the father, I had mixed feelings about Turtle calling home for help. On the one hand, it was funny, but on the other hand, I felt heated and wanted to go down there and shoot the town up. We could spend sometime looking for the niggah that took my son down. Instead, I decided to wire the money to the boy for gas so he could come home. When I walked out of the check-cashing place on Hamilton rd., it was just pass nine PM. I thought about stopping at Jujus to shot some pool over on Broad so I headed that way. I turned on the Broad when I saw the police car comes up from behind. I could tell they were running my plates so I stayed on top of the speed 35mp. When I hit the corner of James and Broad, they hit the lights. As I pulled over, I called Tweet,

"Hey, baby, I may be going to jail tonight, they just pulled me over." I question *"Where you at?"*

"Up on the corner of Broad and James come get my car and I love you"

When she got there my ass was in the back of the police car. I could not talk to her but they did give her my cell phone and the keys to the Road Master. All she could do is blow her man a kiss and take my car home after parking her green convertible over in the pizza shop lot. I sat up until dawn inside the bullpen down town. This would be the first time her man did not come home before the birds started to sing there good morning song to the world, but it won't be the last. This time driving with no-ops got me a seat in the workhouse for ten days before going to court. Tweet will see to it I have whites, money on my books, a visit and keep that pussy tight until I'm home again.

My girl Vicky's beat down

I set in the Hospital pissed about my girl Vicky who lay in bed asleep. The nurse had interred previously took Vicky's vitals then gave her a shot for pain. While she could talk, she told me about the night she got beat. The story for that day was.

At 9:30 pm, she set on the steps of the house she sold from that day. The flow of crack heads had come damn near to a stop. She started to wish I would call or come by and take her out. It has been a little minute, since we spent some time hanging out just the two of us. That was the only time she gets to dress up like a girl in a dress with a purse. Her being out there, getting my money she had to wear sweats to keep up with everything, putting it in many pockets. She wished she had one of them things to bus at a niggah! Maybe a 9mm or a 44 like the one I got with me all the time. But I kept telling her, she needs no gun, every one knows she working for me. To fuck with my shit was to become a dead man walking. Nevertheless, I thought about giving her something to make her feel safer. She said she sat for about a hour when Kim, my number one hoe pulled up with some other bitch asking if she had seen or talked to me to day?

She said, *"No, Why, what's up?"*

Kim got out of the car and stood by her so not to talk loud,

"I haven't talked to him for two days, I been calling and paging, but on answer"

"Well did you call his house?"

"Fuck no; why up set his wife if she aint already up set."

"Fuck that, here make the call" is what she said while she handed her the cell phone.

"Fuck u back bitch I got my own phone" murmur Kim

"Do--u know the number?"

"Yes, thank you" is what she said while pushing the buttons on her cell phone. It rang for a time then she said,

"Hi Miss Tweet, can I talk to Booker, please? O, No, When? How much to get him out? Ok, ok well if and when u talk to him, tell him I got his money put up, and I can put it on his books if he says so. Ok, well can I come with u when he goes to court? Ok, I'll just meet you down there Monday 9 o'clock ok, see you there."

"Damn, he's in jail, they got him Thursday night, and he goes to court on Monday after next and I plan to be there."

"Shit I'm coming too, what court room is it?"

"Don't worry bitch I'll come and get you that morning and we can go together."

To--bad his boy Tech was gone. His funeral was nice, with a lot of slow songs, without many people. Who will look out for Booker Ts shit while he's gone away? It did not take long for the word to get around that Booker T. was locked up out on the pike. Late Saturday night one niggah felt something he

[192]

thought was courage but for real, it was stupidity.

A knock at the door at 3:45Am, Vicky went to answer, as she reached for the doorknob, her inner spirit shouted stop! Her body did just that as the door blow open hitting her in the face. He was on her so fast; aint nothing she could have done. Not even shout out for help, and if she did, who would hear it this time of the night? He dragged her through the hall on into the room tossing her on top of the table like a rag doll. With her lying on her back, he lowered his face to hers to say,

"Where it at bitch; the money, the dope, give it up"

Then he gave her a like Mike, punch into her abdomen. Damn the pain she felt put her in to a ball. She was so small and this niggah was so big. As she relaxed, starting to come out of the ball he hit her again.

"Look, I really aint no killer, but things can happen, you know what I mean?"

By now, Vicky was gasping for air finding it hard to breath. Slowly the lights went out as she went unconscious.

While in that state, she revisited a time when she was eight years old. It was nighttime and she went off to her own bed only to awake in her mother's bed. Her stepfather had transported her into his bed where she laid with nothing on the bottom half of her body. Now she was position with her legs open to him showing a little thing known as, the man in the boat. He is touching it as he contemplates the jail time he will receive if he goes further then touching and licking on this baby. She hears him when he said, *"FUCK IT"* Then she felt a pain she has never felt in her young innocent life. Vicky awakes, into reality, still lying on her back, but she was un-dressed from the waist down and all

[193]

alone. It was hard but she took her time rolling off the top of the table. She held tight to the only chair still standing up right gasping for air while trying to locate her army camouflage jeans. After getting dressed, she headed for home walking as best she could double--over. Her place not too far from the work spot felt good to enter and sit on her own shit. A hot bath was next but she still had trouble breathing while soaking in a hot tub of water. She called Kim to come and help her get over to the hospital. A two-week stay kept Vicky from my court date but it did not keep me from standing beside her bed straight from the courthouse. She had two broken ribs, with one of them piercing her lung; she felt blessed to be alive. Vicky sat quietly in the Road Master, it has been three weeks out of the hospital, and she received her strength back slowly. I had just gone into the store for a cold drink for two. I returned with one grape and one fruit-punch pop. She wanted some chips but there was no eating in my car. It was just about dusk, the Road Master sat still at a red light, when a thing called karma dropped out the sky. Now karma had received the label of payback here in the hood. We never know when it will hit, but we know it will hit one day.   At the red light, Vicky looked over at the car next to us; there she saw the niggah that put her into the hospital. There he was in a car all alone. She wanted to shout out, there's that muthafucka; however, the shock put a knot inside her voice box; all she could do was grab my hand that rested on the armrest. She grabbed hold tighter then ever! I looked over at her and seen the fear on her face,

"What the fuck is up with you?" I asked just as the light changed for the cars to move. All Vicky could do was point franticly! Then her voice came back.

[194]

"That's him! That's that fucker that fucked me up right there!"

"Where at Vicky, which car is it?" I asked

"That one, the blue Ford"

I worked my way behind dude's car. I trailed him over to Smith Rd on the East side. He went inside the parking lot of an apartment complex. I had time to think on what I was going to do to this dude. I must make an example of him that will speak to all dumb-fuckers!

It was dark when we got there .Even darker when dude emerged though the doorway into the parking lot. I stood up against the wall by the door; the light from inside the hall showed me that I had the right man. The niggah walked right pass nodding hello.

When he awakened, he felt himself tied down on the railroad tracks and I had my dick out urinating in his face.

As he moved his head about with an attempt to get the piss out of his eyes he cried out. *"Man please, I'm so sorry, please don't kill me Mr. Booker T. let me make it up some kind of way just don't kill me."*

At that very moment dude knew all the stories he had ever heard about the sick muthafucka name Booker T. was true.

"So you thought you could fuck with mine and nothing would happen to you hah?"

His heart pumped so loud every one could hear it. Vicky stepped closer to the tracks and said, *"I think you need to pay for what you did to me"* she kicked him in the face while adding, *"and I don't mean money!"*

[195]

"So what you thinkin Vicky?, I asked,

"We can leave it all up to you; tell me what you see happening to this piece of shit!"

"Well he fucked me, so how bout I fuck him back, I can use that black night stick in the trunk of the car. It won't kill him, but it will pay him back."

It all sounded good to me but I had to ask dude,

"Well dude what you think about that being her payment to you?"

He wasted no time agreeing to the ass fucking, at least he will be alive to deny the story if Vicky ever told someone. I untied him from the track and tied him over the hood of my Road Master.

"Niggah I'm telling you now! If you get shit on my car you will have to pay me and you aint gone like my fee."

Vicky got started and put damn near the whole thing in that niggah ass hole it took every bit of four minutes with her moving not so slow then it was over.

"Know this dude! You got off easy!"

Dude got himself together while saying,

"I know man! Thank you and believe me, you won't ever see me again! I swear!"

Then we all got back into the Road Master. Vicky seated in the back still unsatisfied. I drove taking dude back to his car, as he got out and softly closed my car door, I reached under the seat and got out my sawed-off shotgun. I called him back over. As he approached the car, I put one into his kneecap taking off half of his leg. While he yelled cries of bloody murder, I said,

"That there's for messing with my shit niggah!"

[196]

Then Road Master pealed away while dude held on to his short leg shouting, "W*hy man! Why!"*

Wherever I take me, there I am:

If I get dope inside my body, I had to put it there:

If getting high was the answer then what was the question:

A Second Honeymoon

I knew my husband Booker T. felt really bad about the thing that happen with LiL Don scamming us and we have not had a lot of time together lately. Being the romantic he is, he came into our crib at two in the morning and stood over the bed where I'm sleeping quietly. He reached down and snatched back the thick sky-blue comforter while calling my name with added orders to get up and put something on. I did as told putting back on the blue jeans and white top from earlier today. He sat on the end of the bed looking at my every move throughout the room. When I was fully dressed, he took my hand and led me out of the house to his Road Master. *"So where are we going baby?"* I ask but he never answered. He opened my door for me to enter the car, and then he softly closed it behind me. For a short time, he just looked in through the window at me. He smiled as if it were the first time he had really seen me. It was not until I seen the sign high way I76 North did he say,

"Tweet I love u so much and we need some time to our self so sit back and enjoy the ride please."

That was just what I did with no more questions, as the car blew down the road I read the up coming signs. At some point, I went off to sleep. I awoke at a Niagara Falls sign. He parked at a five star hotel and he went in to check us in. When Booker T. returned to the car, a bellhop stepped up and asked if we had bags. My wonderful husband spoke up and said "not now but we will when we check out thank u for asking."

He opened my car door reached his hand down to help me step out. Thinking

O-my-God, I reached out placing my hand into his and stepped out with all the grace of a black Queen! He acquired an upper level suite; we stepped off the elevator on to the plushest red carpet I have ever set foot on. When we got to our door, Booker T. said, "don't move baby!" I stood at the door while he opened it up. Swoop and I was up into his arms. Once again, he looked me deep into my eyes and said, *"I love you Tweet"* with that, he stepped into the room kicking the door closed behind him. In the center of the living room, he stood still holding me in his arms. Then he dropped my legs and held on to my waist allowing me to rap my dangling free legs around his waist. My arms locked around his neck now we are face to face with large happy smiles' on them. He continued to hold his smile while declaring,

"Today is officially Tweet day, so what is it my love you would like to do?"

It did not take me long to come up with something out of our past.

"Well dear Sr. if you would be so kind as to take me into the bed room over to the bed and set me down."

Booker T. nodded his head once before saying,

"If that is your wish sweet Tweet it is done!"

He then walked into the next room over to a large king size bed, with at lest fifteen different shaped pillows that covered the top. Believe me when I say there are no words to enlighten you the reader to how I felt at that time. The love I felt at that moment no! No, it is the fact of knowing how much he is in love with me that gave me the goose bumps all over my body. He doesn't just love me he is in love with me. Not every wife can claim she still feels that coming from her man! He placed me at the foot of the bed where I quickly got

[200]

up on my knees. Facing him I started to undress him as I told him of my joy with pillow talk .We have not had that for a long time and that is my wish right now. With his shirt and sweats off, he stood there before me in his C. K. boxers looking fine as fuck, I jokingly ask,

"Well u gone undress me or do I have to wish for that too?" Booker T. head went back as he had a good laugh. Then he got under way removing my top and jeans. Then we pulled up to the top of the bed and started to talk.

"Ok Tweet what's on your mind?" he softly asked.

"Well first I would like to call truth if that is ok with u."

"Very well, truth it is," he declared.

I love to call truth with my husband because that's the one time he cannot lie to me in an attempt to save my feeling from the pain of the truth. However, I best not ask for more then I can handle.

"First truth, remember when you gave that fat ass bitch Onya a ride to the hospital and then you stayed with her the whole time."

"Yes"

"Did u or did u not tell her she could be your outside girl!"

"Hell no! First off that bitch onya looks like she got five assess' humped up on her back with her knees knocking when she walk, I can't sell shit like that! However, I did get my dick sucked baby four at--least two or three days in a row. She was praying I would fuck her big ass but I never did on truth I swear!"

"But after we went through the shit with Mo from the recovery rooms in the beginning of our relationship we said no fucking around inside the rooms."

"Ok, but we also agreed that if a bitch in the recovery world gone suck my dick I was gone let her and you was cool with that. Shit Onya talked all this good suck a dick when we was at the hospital then when she got her mouth on it the bitch didn't know how to chock she kept fighting it so I said fuck it and got ghost"

Hearing his answers allowed me to snuggle up into his arms a little more. Now it's his turn and he asked about a stay over at my sponsors house was it truly just seven ladies camping out with popcorn and DVD's?

"Yes baby that is all it was but it was seven females not ladies because three of them were lesbians." That comment opened an outpour of laughter. I want to ask if he were fuckin them hoe's that work for him but I was afraid of the answer I may get from him. If he tells me yes, I wouldn't want him pimping no longer. Fuck that shit I cannot let bullshit end this good time so I changed my line of thinking and we just talked and laughed all day about whatever until darkness hit the windows.

I seat up on the side of the bed call room service, while I waited for the pick up I look, back to see my husband fast asleep so I hung up the phone. I seat and looked at him while he slept his peaceful sleep and could see the little boy inside him. Then I walked round this large elegant breath-taking place. A panorama scene was set in every room.

The bedroom offered a trip into the wild African lands with wallpaper giving the representation of open land with lions strolling freely. Brown and gold satin covered the bedding and windows. Placed through out the room a number of African clay pottery's along with a number of large banana plants. The floors are high glossed wood with three large lion fur throw rugs with the head intact.

Slowly I looked around as I stood and walked to a set of tall bubble mahogany doors. They stood halfway open, with arms out stretched I pushed. Egyptian scene position before me in the living room. With all the excitement arriving I did not see it. Now fully into the room, I can see the overall of it. Wallpaper covering three walls showed formation of the Egyptian pyramid. On the west Nile bank. Ancient by gold hooks that grip lit--sticks with little bulbs' of soft lighting illuminating the room. I took a seat on the black leather sofa. A dark cheery wood oval shaped table stood in front and on both sides. Each table Egyptian vases filled with White roses. A huge painting of Anubis the mythological god of death boldly hung over an immense marble mantle below it a fireplace. I sat and allowed my mind to roll play with what it may have been like for a black person back then with the sun cooking the shit out of everyone's skin in Egypt. For a time I sat and tripped about how good a black person may have fit into the crowd until they spoke out. Thinking of the looks they got had me laughing so hard I damn near pissed myself.

Quickly I jumped to my feet and ran for the bathroom. Running straight through the bedroom on into the bathroom, no time to pull down my thong, I just sat down on the toilet. I did try to pull the string over to the side but it still got wet.

"Ok it's a good time to take a bath" Are the words that whispered out my

[203]

mouth?

Seated on the toilet my eyes open to the marvel of this room.

The onyx covers the floor here the stone color lines more to a sky blue. The walls are pearl white up to the border which was gold trim above that was a powder blue ceiling painted over it are a number of cotton white clouds giving an open sky look. In the center of the room are steps going down into the floor for the bath. Damn It looks like I'm inside a Roman bath house with two gold fountains coming out of the wall over to my right, clearly it's a his and her showers enclosed by one large glass case. The left wall fully cover by a looking glass with his and her sink. Nice size gold fountains for the faucet coming up and out over the sinks. Coming up out the floor are gold foot paddles for the hot and cold-water control. Spaced throughout the room are long white candles so I light them all and turn on the water for the step down tub. Over by the door a stand full of towels and a number of glass jars full of different color bath salts to sooth and refresh the air.

"*Damn! I must be close to heaven*" are my words as I lay back into the bubbly hot water. A dope fiend like me enjoying a place like this one here, God Is good. I close my eyes to enjoying the moment. As I do so, my diseased thinking kicks in.

While humbleness is the best state of mind for a addict I can not help but to thanked God for being here at this time.

Nonetheless, the job of the disease is to keep me down in spirit. How dear I feel good about something nice happening to or for me. With that, my mindset moved to the reality of who was paying for this trip. Truth was the pain of many people paid for this shit. The many men and women that cried all through the night because here love one never came home with their paycheck. Children in the world going to bed starving. Food stamps sold to get one more high. All the ways and means a person will and have used to get more dope shot through my mine before I began to think; no-no- to question; the coldness inside a person taking the money from these people. Thinking of coldness in my husband, I must have been thinking to hard because I began to hear my name called.

"In here."

I shouted as I continued to enjoy my hot bath with my eyes closed. Soon I felt his body as he slowly slide down in front of me. He leaned back to rest against me as my eyes popped open.

There we soaked enchanted by the flicking candles until I said,

"Baby, I could have never in a hundred years envisioned something like this. Thank you for all this."

"Tweet you put up with so much everyday from me with the bitchies, late night runs sometimes I think to say how much I love u but, shit be happening so fast, I lose the time and the word's while on the path of getting that money! If you will bear with me a little longer it will all be over."

"What u saying Booker"

"I'm saying I'm tired of this shit baby, I'm saying we can take the money I got put away and do some legal legit shit for once."

Booker T. extended his hand for mine to join his, I placed my palm on top of his and together we said the anthem that we have stood on for nine years running.

"Baby through life or death I'm with you, no matter what goes down, I aint going no where!"

My arms wrap around my husband and I held on tight. After we looked wrinkled, a bit we got out of the water and called room service for some food. When the food was done our day was done and sleep came quick to use. The morning came with a hot breakfast we ordered the night before. After a good shower, we got dressed and went shopping for clothing for the next two days. Back to the room for a change of clothes and back out. We walk the streets holding hands like new lovers deep in love. Time passed fast and it was the last night here, my plan was to give my husband the A- game sex. I went into the bathroom to get that ass hole set for entry.

Ladies the one thing about ass hole fucking is clean that thing out first he last thing a man wants is brown stuff on his dick! So get started about noon and take a laxative to get ready for the fun you will have that night. Standing inside the bathroom, I place the bottle of Flees enemas inside of my ass. Having prepared myself, I place a nice amount of lube in and around my ass hole; this will cut some of the pain during entry. When I felt ready to have my man inside of my ass, I went back into the bedroom.

I started at his knees kissing my way up to that big dick. I spend time showing him throat choking love {relax the throat and let the dick slide in deeper} the sound of me choking makes his dick hard as hell. Next, I set on top of his dick and slowly work the head into my ass humping up and down easy like. O-shit he has started to hump acting hungry to get up inside my butt. My full stop of the hip movement coincides with the grabbing hold of his neck to get his attention. Then I said something tasteful like.
"If you plan to live pass this fuck I suggest you slow your roll niggah!"
With out a word his stillness allows me to do my thing. Before long, it's in and I'm ridding a wild horse at the rodeo.
Damn! That shit was good but he needs to have some control, it's a man thing as if he's missing some ass-hole. For that reason, over I go on my back. My legs set to a gymnast spilt. He feels at home now, all up in that ass hole. I can always tell when he ready to shoot by the sound he makes.

[207]

O-yes, he's ready and I love this part because he jumps up standing over me to shoot cum all over me. I call it cum shower.

Sleep always comes quick for two sex beaten lovers and that was what we were at that time.

"Good morning Tweet" Were the whispered words in my ear at six A.M.?

"Come on baby we got to get on the road!"

With our things packed into one bag, we are on our way home. Why is it the ride home is always quicker then the ride out of town? Is it, our joy in talking about the good time we had at the waterfall? We got so close when we got on a boat ride in the splashing water without a raincoat. We had a great time along with renewing the fact that we don't just love but we are in love with each other. While we where gone the grand jury called for an indictment on Booker T. and now it is about the waiting game for us. The state will not spend money looking for him. The law of average says he will go to jail on a humbug one day.

NEED SOME DOPE

Turtles back in the Co and feeling some kinda way about dude pounding him on the head. (Pay back is a bitch!) His had to stop putting men down on the ground and his gut felt twisted in knots for just one job. Nevertheless, he remembered his dad's words and he gave his word that his son won't put muthafuckers down on the ground. Moreover, Turtle knew what would happen if he did not stand by that word. He calls home hopping to get someone to cosign his bullshit thinking.

"Mom not pulling stick ups are hard! I keep seeing men leaving them-selves wide-open for the take down."

"Baby boy I'm telling you the real, If you think you can handle the shit on the other side of that door then turn the knob and walk the fuck on in. However don't cry after that door closes and your bad ass can't get the fuck out" That was the best I could give him other then telling him I love you no matter what you do.

Turtle took his dope he had left from out of town and went to work. It did not take long for him and his best friend $tink-boy, to sell out. They had their money but it could be better.

"Turtle said,

"Damn, $tink-boy we got stacks between us but, this will not do it. What we need to go back to Altoona and get that big pay and I'm talking big boy money. Nevertheless, to get it, we need some big ass money. I was thinking, how bout doing some stick-ups. We can hit some of the fast food spots, like Mc

[209]

Dees or Captain Burger. If we time it right just before closing the money should be good."

Don't get it wrong my son Turtle had money stacked inside shoe boxes down inside my house, some where I' m not suppose to know about ,nevertheless that is no-touch money. He put it up for whenever funky shit goes down and he needs it to live on so not to be a burden on no one. He never thinks about that money when he is in need of more money.

First thing Turtle did was check out some spots, stopping in to get a feel while ordering some fries, and talking to the manager about a job opening. Ok, he got a spot so the next time he gets water and the managers phone number. It took him a week of sexing this ugly ass bitch. Now she's helping him hit her own store. It went down on a Sunday night; the store was full of the weekend take. Turtle knew where the safe and the video tapes were located. This take plus what he already had, put him up to eleven stacks. Good but know one will fuck with him on the sale of some dope. Pull out a large amount of dope in front of Turtle and not cry about it later. There was not a niggah in the City of Columbus that had a level of intelligence that low, the phone call for help started out

"Dad I need help, can we meet at the house and talk about it, say half an hour from now?"

Book T. thought about it for a second then he said, *"Ok, I'll see you there."*

Turtle got to the house early hoping to find something good inside refrigerate. I saw my baby boy was hungry so I made him some cheese eggs, hotcakes and bacon. By the time Booker T.'s feet hit the doorway, he could still smell the food, except the food was all gone. That meant I had to turn the stove back on, and do it all over again, While I cooked, the men took a seat in Booker T.'s poolroom in the basement.

"So tell me what's going on with you son?"

"Shit, and more shit, man, dad, I got money, but won't anybody sell me anything. I need your help to get ten stacks of shit. Some green, some boy and some of that good hard."

Booker T. thought on it for a time as he started hitting some balls around the pool table. Then he said,

"Ok, give me a day to set it up, then I will take you to get it. Now I don't need to tell you if you go back and hit this dud up, I won't be able to help you out of it. You under stand what I'm saying to you Turtle?" While looking his dad in the eyes Turtle responded, *"Yes, sir, I got where you coming from."*

Just then, I called down the steps, telling my husband to come eat.

It took two days, to talk LiL Don into letting Turtle come to his home to spend ten stacks. The saying, the apple don't fall far from the tree is true, even though Turtle was not my natural born son, we are still just a like in a lot of ways. One of them ways is when it comes time to take care of business that is what we do. All that pussy-ass, playing around, will get you killed or fucked the fuck up if you dumb enough to come where men are getting together acting like a little boy. That type of shit will get your ass whipped for sure. My son and I arrived at LiL Don's crib at 10AM. The two of us stepped up to

[211]

the door and knock not too hard but a respectable knock. There is no answer, we looked at each other and then I knocked just a tad harder

"What the fuck u knocking on my door like that for? Like you the police or somethin."

That's what we can hear coming from the other side of the door, along with the turning of at-lest five locks click, click-click. Finally, the door opened. Lil Don acted insecure peeping past the two of us.

*"Come on in, you muthafucka knocking like you the police, I should have just started shootin that thing out through the damn doo*r."

Move the fuck out the way dude so we can get in, scary ass niggah!" is what I said as we pushed past him on into the crib. The two of us take a seat at the dinning room table while LiL Don was still standing talking shit to my son.

"So you the little niggah that had the C/O shaking in their boots; Ha, you, don't, look, like a killer!"

I broke in and said,

"Stop the talking and get to working, we came here for a reason and listening to you aint it."

"Ok, Ok you got the money, I got the dope"

Turtle stood pulled out his money, and placed it on the table and sat back into his seat. Lil Dons dumb grabs up the money off the table and started bull shittin again.

"Where you get this type of money young buck? Shit, I got your money now; you can get the fuck out and, thank you for doing business."

Before LiL Don, could start to laugh showing he was playing. Turtle was

[212]

standing with that thing pointed at LiL Don's face. There was no need for words from Turtle

LiL Don instantly called for help from me.

"Book, Book man, get your boy, man this shit here aint funny; pointing that thing at me" *"Fuck niggah, you started this shit; you know better then to play with a niggah and his money! Say you don't know, that shit will get you dead quicker then shit."* Lil Don sounded sick when he asked,

"No joke man gets your kid"

I stepped beside Turtle and placed my hand on his shoulder then I said,

"Don't call on me nigga, you best be callin on God now?"

LiL Don nicely set the money down on the table and Turtle nicely, took a step back, and sat down in his seat. His gun placed on his lap, finger still inside the trigger. Then Turtle spoke his first words sense entering the crib.

"Look dude, or Mr. LiL Don, I came here to buy some dope, not to test my man hood. Now, if you just need to see my nuts, to find out just how big they are, I got no problem pulling them out. However, if I do, only one of us will live to tell this story and I always tell the best stories. From here, the best thing that can happen is you sell me some dope and I leave or I take my money off the table and leave. But know it's, only because my father is here, that I don't kill you and take my money along with all your dope and money, after I cook and eat some of your food."

All this said with coldness in Turtles eye that shock the fuck out of LiL Don. My fast talk stopped the smell of death in the air.

"Come on guys, it aint that serious!"

[213]

LiL Don broke eye contact while laughing, *"Yup, it aint, but we do need to end this get together, so, what was it you wanted."*

The business went off right and my son and I jumped into the Road Master with the dope. While riding down the street I told my son just how proud of him I was for not letting a niggah talk down to him. Then I went on to say,

"In this life as black men all we got other then a good lady by our side, is a first impression and that is how one man will or will not remember you. And that short ass fucka right there will always remember you with respect."

Turtle nodded his head while taking it in as "Food for thought." Back at his boys crib, we talked more about the two of them taken their act on the road back to Altoona. This time Turtle will not be slippin. I continued to chill with LiL Don off and on. From time to time received questions as to where Turtle was and how was he doing. I have always talked boastful about my son when talking of him. Turtle called me, told me he did not need to fuck with LiL Don any more. He hooked up with his cousin Slim in Pittsburgh, Pa.

While chillin inside the club in Pittsburgh $tink-boy got into a fight with some dude over a piece of ass. The police came ran a 50 on every body, too bad he had an Ohio warrant that came up so off to jail $tink-boy went.

Turtle cousin Slim, seen all the big-money Turtle was getting out of town and decided to eat big time. He joins in on the next run. Slim a 20-year-old light brown man stands 6, 2 straight up and down. He's the baby boy to Tweets little sister. These to Niggah's are super close, as brothers' people that don't know call them brothers. Now these two brothers are getting money

[214]

without $tink-boy, O--yes eating off a big plate, full of money.   Turtle had a high-speed chase with the po-po one night. Grand theft auto was what he played with the po-po up and down the streets on the north side of Pittsburg. It started on the top of Charles Street and Federal extensions. My son and I had been on the phone when he said,

"Hold on dad I got a sale."

He made a crack sale out of the truck window and the police seated in their car seen it. They hit the lights and Turtle took off not because of the dope he had on him but it was the gun inside slims truck that forced him to keep it moving. Now back on the phone with me he said,

"Dad, you may not believe this, but the cops hit the lights on me and I'm on the run. I got 2 twenties and a 44 with cop killer bullets on me.

A minatory five years in the pen if they snag me now so I got to go."

Up one street and back down another Turtle went. Thinking quickly he pulled in between two other trucks and hit the lights. The police car flew pass not seeing him parked there and turned right at the corner and went down the hill. Turtle pulls out gets to the same corner and turns left up the hill. He runs into some other police car coming down. Now he had to play chicken with the police their heading straight at each other. Heart to play chicken inside a truck is something everybody aint got. However, Turtle had it that night as he floored the gas and did not stop or turn away. The police car forced over into a parked car! A loud bang made on lookers from the houses. Them police was pissed about that and if they could have got their hands on my son I know they would have beat him bad if not killed him. Having got pass that police car Turtle hit one corner and then enough getting up to speeds of 75 or 80 on side streets. Real shit, that nigga did a lot of talking to the gangster god until he parked across the street from Slims grandfather's house. Moving even quicker, he jumped out the truck and ran into the crib. The police found the truck but there was no one inside it nor did the tags go to a house on this street. Door to door, the police knocked asking, "*Who drives that Ford truck?*" I think you know there wasn't an answer at Slims grandfather's house when the police knocked. The police towed the truck away with no charges given to the owner, who was at work. There was no proof of who was driving that night. Yes, truck stolen from the work parking lot. It cost a bit to get that truck back but Turtle had it and came out of pocket with it. Slim did not think it funny at all getting his peeps truck caught up in something with the police. From there Turtle had to drive his own car to get around in Pittsburg.

Turtle Goes To Jail

Can't say why Turtle started fucking with that bitch Nicky again but he did. On the day of his take down by the police, Turtle just got into town driving his own car. Turtle, Slime and Nicky are riding through the town of Altoona looking for a fiend that called Nicky to deliver three grams of powder. Down 13th Street they traveled when the police hit five cars deep like swat, they surrounded the car cutting it off. One fat cop shouted, *"driver turn off the car and let us see your hands."*

Turtle did as told while five other police rushed the windows with their guns pointed inside. Turtle thinking quick after the dope and his gun where found up under the hood of his car. Said,

"Slim was just getting a ride he aint got nothing to do with nothing."

No need for both men to go to jail about this shit however this bitch Nicky O—yes this was his chance to pay this bitch back for that stick up/ lick she had put on him before. He told the police,

"What ever you have found belongs to the girl and me."

First, write up in the Newspapers

Drug task force deters alleged operation

Officers stopped a car late Monday after a confidential informant said Turtle 19, of Columbus Ohio would be in town, what his car looked like and how he had, every thing hid under the hood of his car next to the battery. $11,000 will come from the sale of heroin, crack, and powder cocaine. A semi-automatic

[217]

handgun, plastic bags housing marijuana and a scale. The District Attorney said the 94 grams of cocaine could bring a three-year mandatory prison term, and he is considering request for a mandatory two-year sentence because of the school zone violation even those police stopped the car near an elementary school. The 100 packets of heroin found in the car also could lead to mandatory two-years in prison in all turtle could face seven-years of mandatory time. The following is the breakdown of drugs seized early Tuesday after a vehicle stop in the area of 13th Street and 13th Avenue

62.6 grams of crack cocaine

Street value 5,000;

32.5 grams of powder cocaine, street value 2,500;

100 packets of heroin, labeled "Happy Holidays"

Street value 4,000;

Happy Holidays' dealer sentenced Ohio man caught in December with bags of heroin gets 2 to 4 years in state prison. A Columbus, Ohio man caught last December with a stash of drugs, including 100 bags of heroin stamped "Happy Holidays", Will spend 2 to 4 years in state prison. Judge sentenced 19-year-old Turtle to the mandatory minimum jail time for selling drugs in a drug-free school zone. He is eligible for participation in a boot camp for inmates. Drug Task Force agents and police officers arrested Turtle and two others companions Dec.21 downtown a confidential informant told drug agents and police that Turtle and his friends would be transporting drugs under the hood of a vehicle. Police found a black bag wedged beside the battery of Turtles vehicle.

Damn! My son made the news top story .All that dope. Is that how they do it in Columbus Ohio? That dude Turtle! Done gone out with a bang? That is about all Turtles friends had to say, no one had a dime on his bail money 10% of 125,000. I'm feeling some kind of way inside. My baby-boy gone and I can't do nothing but write letters of hope, words of guidance and put some money on his books. My husband could have put the money out there for bail or attorney, but he said going to jail is part of the game. Some times, we win and some times, we lose. However, we must play the game through to become a better man in life. If Turtle is as smart as I think, he'll get all he can get out of the programs offered and never go back. That is back to the dope game or back to jail. The first week I spent every night on my knees praying,

"Lord please, let no man born out of woman harm my son, please put a armor around him and keep him safe from all weapons made by man in Jesus name I pray." I sent Turtle a letter asking if he needed me to get that money he had put up. He wrote back no because he will need it when he get home.

I did not understand how the police knew of him being in town to get money at that time or how they knew about his hiding spot under the hood. Then I read the Altoona press; Fuck ass informant I wished I knew who it was, but after putting to and too together I knew it was that hating ass marked man.

On a personal, note separate from the body of this work. I would like to thank all the guards down inside FCI Gilmore Prison for being so nice to me and mine whenever we came down to visit my husband. Booker T. Braddy 66945-061

Booker T.'s

Living Sucker Free

The two guns and different types of dope found inside my husband car, the grand jury called for an indictment on him. Two years, he had to set real still staying sucker free. He kept his girls but sold the club, for no-where near what it was worth. Bitch ass LiL Don, felt overly, fired up he did not get his hands on the club. It was late fall, on a Friday evening that Booker T. and I sat back chillin looking at old moves, eating popcorn. We heard the horn of LiL Don's car blow. Booker T. stepped out front then came back in and said,

"I'll be right back, the men need to holla at me."

That was the last time I saw my husband as a free man. It took God himself to get me up off the floor after I listened to LiL Don tell the story through the cell phone.

"Tweet I'm sorry man but Booker T. is in the back of the police car man. I was playing with the damn cop up here at the gas station. I jumped out of the car saying these guys are trying to kidnap me; help! Next thing I know the cop got his gun pulled out and he putting every one on the ground then he ran a 50 on every body and Booker is the only one that did not get to go home. I wish there was something I could do or say to help Tweet. Damn man I'm so sorry about this whole thing"

O-yes, it took God himself to lift me off the floor but no one or nothing but time could stop me from crying. The words keep replaying inside my head like a move replaying repeatedly with little twist and turns in it.

"Booker is gone man."

"What! What the fuck are you talking about Don?"

"Tweet, Booker is in the back of the cop car man he's on his way down

[222]

town."

"What happen?"

"I pulled up in the Gas station on Livingston, in back of a cop car and I got out playing around saying help these guys is trying to jack me. Next--thing I know, the fucka is pulling out his gun and telling ever body to get out of the car and get on the ground. I tried to tell him I was just playing around but he started running 50's on every body and every one was cool but Booker. His future indictments must be in. Man I'm sorry Tweet but there was nothing we could do. I wish I never did that shit I don't know what made me play around like that."

Ok, I have a question for you the reader.

"How many of you plays around with the police?"

Come on this shit had to be a set up. The only car in the gas station was the cop car until LiL Don pulled up, and then there were only the two cars. That was the last day I saw my husband as a free man. Some days I can hear him say, *"I'll be right back baby as he kissed me"*

"Hold up niggah! Where u going" I asked,

"Just gone to make a quick run with Don and Head they want to talk about something."

I'm holding on to him while I said,

"But you don't fuck with them no more, so why you going?"

He pulled free kissed me and went out the door.

I went straight sick crying all day and night holding on to his pillow trying to smell him in everything while I wished it was him. I even went through the

[223]

dirty clothes smelling his things and holding them close to my face as I cried out his name. Still I cry some nights longing for him to be home with me.

We spent his county jail time together, which worked out to nearly one year. Jailhouse visits twice a day put me through some of the dumpiest shit I have every gone through in my life. The visiting room is cute into an L shape! The sign in

Window is one small wall while the longer wall is made of thick glass where the intakes Deputies sat and looked at the line of people. A number of viewing monitors and computers and other things needed to keep track of the inmates sat inside that room. Across from that are steps closed in by a large gate opening only for polices officers to enter. An elevator lifted family and friends up to one of the five-visitor floors. The afternoon parking was impossible so nighttime visit work best. It started at six pm, with free parking on the street starting at the same time. I had fights over parking spaces a number of times because I was up in there to see mine. I could have done the pay parking but the money I save from parking went to my husbands books. A single visitor's sign up line started lining up at five thirty. Come six o'clock that line of standing people went from the sign in window back up around the corner to the door in an L shaped. After a while of coming and standing in line, I started meeting other people there to see their love ones. We talked small talk about kids, jobs and magazines we traded for our peeps however that first time visiting was the kicker. I Step off the elevator into a small oblong room. At my left was a wall my right showed six small square thick glass windows. A small partition wall set between the windows to offer some type of privacy. I stood there wandering where the guards where. A person points toward the left of me while telling me to go place the visit slip up against the glass of the first window. The window in front of me had a number six on it so I fallowed the numbered windows down to the one where I found the guard desk inside of it. I held the paper up then pressed it to the glass. He looked at the pass then wrote something in a logbook. Then he told me what window to wait at for the inmate. O-boy, how my heart jumped inside of my chest as I stood in front of that window waiting for the guard to bring my boo. Finally the guard came with him and pulled open that heavy gate so he could step inside for me to see. Booker steps inside that cell moving close up to the glass our hands went up at the some time giving an attempt to touch each other's hands through that thick glass. While looking into each other's eyes our lips say I love you. As we talked through the glass, I wanted to show my man some tits or some ass. It had been two weeks since they let me see him and I wanted to see his dick. After I saw the lay out of the county jail, I got a bright idea of how to bring my man some pussy ever time I come to see him. If I timed it, right I would get window 5 or 6 down at the far end. We will only have twenty minuets at best thirty so there was no time to waste on little kid head games shit. After a time of talking, I pulled out my portable DVD player from my pocketbook. Open it and push play. Booker T. had with him up--under his shirt a towel tucked into his paints and hair grease cuffed inside his hand for lube. This helps get his shit off with out getting a brush burn on his pretty dick. While he shot that nut he looked into my eyes and say,

"I love you."

Two girls with a man worked best for him, looking at some real pussy and real dick sucking kept Booker T. happy as hell while locked down. Damn! I would give my left tit to hold him inside my arms and allow him to kiss me the way only he can kiss me. See ladies it is not everyday that a woman can meet her soul mate in life. I've had a number of men that I let go of due to them going into the prison. So what is different about my husband? The first thing is he is my husband second never in my life have I loved a man as I do him. Whenever the pain of not being with him is stronger, them the pain of going through his bullshit; I knew I had to hold on one more day. Therefore, if you know he loves you hold on a change is gone come. As for me I never missed a visit at the county jail, visiting two times per week keeping money on his books plus showing the coldest porn DVDs inside the jail house to my boo.

Fed Sentence Day

It had to be about 6:30AM when my eyes opened for the fourth time since going to bed last night. Sleep just doesn't come easy for me with Booker T. locked up in jail. Today I got butterflies moving all around inside of my gut from anticipation of the up coming sentencing today. 9 o'clock Federal court for my husband, and I'm praying he will get 3 to 5 but Federal time has never been that short unless a fucker tells on someone. His Attorney was talking the possibility of him with 20 to 30 years unless he takes the plea bargain of 10 years. Even thou this was his first number. Booker T. Attorney said it don't matter because he got two gun charges and two dope/ possession(green and crack) with intent, and each gun has a mandatory sentence by it self. Shit aint no telling what he will get for the intent. The prosecutor was shooting for the reecho-act, which will give him life.

Come on ladies get up, court won't wait for us to get there before it starts. Kim and Vicky slept over at my house so we can all go to court together in one car. Then I still have to get my mother in-law from the hotel. She came into town late last night and got herself a room out by the airport. I must move my butt if I plan to be at court on time. I pulled out from home at 8AM. Twenty after my mother in-law was in my car. Mother this is Kim and this is Vicky very good friends of Booker T. and me. I felt no need to tell her the real about the women that they work for your son. I can hear it now, question after question and I know these ladies love my husband in there own way and right now he is in need of all the love and support he can get. Yes, I am hurting also but this is not about me it is about his happiness on whatever level he can find it. His knowing the three of us are holding each other up will keep him stress

[228]

free. Seated inside the courtroom, I heard a lot of shit I did not understand coming from the judge other then him asking Booker T. did he have something to say. He said yes then made his first apology to his mother, for being a let down, standing here before her like this.

Then to me his Wife, asking for forgiveness, for taking away time that he should have spent giving me joy. Then he spoke to the courts asking for forgiveness for being of burden to them. There was not a dry eye in the courtroom during that time. Then the Judge gave him 110 months = just short of 10 years. All of us cried while the deputy took him back out the courtroom with his shackles jingling. Our walk back to my car quit with every ones chest full of emotions! My mother in-law full of emotions and questions asked,

"So tell me just what happen with this guy LiL Don and Booker going to jail. Was he even there in the court room today?"

My face twisted up as I remembered just who I was about to talk to. Catching myself I stopped the cuss words that were forming inside my mouth from coming out. My face continued to be twisted but my tone was soft as I said,

"Did LiL Don Come to court to offer his support, is that what you are asking me, mother?"

"Hell no mother, this niggah LiL Don has been running around telling a story of how Booker T. was tired of the game and gave himself over to the police on the day he went to jail." Mother's voice went up a tone as she asked,

"Get real, what niggah! Wants to go to jail?" The three ladies sit back quit in the car riding back to my house as I told my mother in-law parts of this story she don't know.

[229]

"Look mom the whole thing about this is Booker T. should never have been in a Fed Cell from the start, at best he should be doing probation for the State with one gun in addition to one dope possession with intent. The code (We don't talk to the police) is what your son was living by when the police pulled over his car. LiL Don Nephew Paul and a book bag he placed into the back seat helped to do Booker T. in on that day. After a time the police questioned "whose book bag is this?" Booker T. did not tell. He never believed in telling on a friend and that is his down fall."

Mother asked,

"So if that was his friend why did he not step up and be a man and say, "this is my bag."

What I told mother was this.

"Booker T. and Paul went off to jail that day. He kept waiting for this so-called friend to say something to save him but it never did happen. Ten days later and Booker T. is home from the workhouse now feeling some kind of way about this whole thing. He keeps thinking, "Damn I know this niggah aint gone let me take the fall for his bag?" Paul aint saying shit about it, but he still comes around the club chilling like it just didn't happen. Therefore, my husband came right out with it

"Dude, what are you gone do about that bag?" Paul spoke up,

"What bag, that shit belong to my uncle that was not mine"

In disbelief Booker T. questioned,

"Who are you talking about, LiL Don?"

Paul not trying to take the blame said,

[230]

"Hell yeah, he had me drop it off up north for him and you was the ride."

"What are you saying Tweet" asked mother

"I don't know mom I guess Booker T. trusted LiL Don and now he will do 10 years."

My mother in laws was sad sounding when she said,

"Man that is deep stuff Tweet and all we can do is continuing to call upon God to keep his arms around Booker T. and bring him home safe."

Those words coming from my mother in laws left the car pretty quit all the way back to the airport. She and I both got out the car while she said her well-mannered good byes to Vick and Kim I took the pleasure of gettin her bags from the back of the car. We stood and hugged holding on to each other for a time while we cried. Our feelings of lose overflowed within us both as we whispered I love you, took in a deep breath and let go of each other. My mother in-law went back to Baltimore where she has fifteen years clean and works helping recovering addicts in treatment. The girls and I stopped for a bite to eat and then went to my house. They stayed with me for about a week consoling each other over late night coffee and frustrated conversations. These ladies have the ability to do other things with their lives however; can't choose one with out Booker T. telling them what to do. Old habits die-hard and they still felt a need to go and get that money for my husband. O-no sweet ladies Booker T. and I have to walk this walk together just the two of us. The best advice I could tell Kim and Vicky was move on in your life. Go and use whatever you got from my husband and keep going to a better life at the end! I hugged Kim and Vicky good-bye at my front door. That was our last day

[231]

together. I get a call from time to time just to say hello. The last call from Vicky was last year and she was attending Columbus State Collage. I did have a letter from Kim too she is up state doing time for prostitution and she went back to smoking crack. I honestly wish the best for all these ladies may they find a happy trail to travel.

Ok now to you the reader tell me what you think. Come to roxannefredd@yahoo.com and talk to me because I know who the fuck the marked man is and I got something for his ass.

Journal entry **5**

Mr. Journal, I can't do much more of this bullshit. Sitting alone inside the car with self is the worst thing in the world for a recovering addict like me. It's getting easy for me to listen to me about something I don't really want to think of. As I blame myself for the fucked up life my son turtle lived that took him away in jail. If I were a better mother, he never would have gone gangster. Maybe his life would have worked out some other way, if I were not on dope when he was a young boy shit, MAYBE, MAYBE. Fuck that! Choices make champions! He is who he is and I did school him on right from wrong. I can't let that shit get me down. The marked man went up in the chicken spot; gettin them good chicken wings. I wish I had some chicken was my thought while I look through the bottom of my pocketbook for some gum or something to chew on, shit a bitch was getting hungry on these long nights. Hold up what is this I have found, too old ass letters. One from my son Turtle and one from my sweet boo. I re-read them and could hear the sound of there voice inside my head. I felt fucked up for the rest of the night just feeling bad from being all alone; through watery eyes Turtles letter read.

Hi mom,
I'm ok in here, so don't go stress. Mom I do care about freedom and you know I'm sorry bout fuckin up this time and can't get out with out seeing a Little

time down. However, I will be ok. Mommy you know I didn't have no money for envelope or food by me just getting here, but look, a friend from Pittsburgh, looked out for me. I didn't have much, but I played dice with all of it and I won a lot of shit. Therefore, you know, what happen, Niggah's was mad and things got bad, I stabbed a niggah! 7 times, so now I'm back in the hole again, but this time for 90 days, Mom I'm trying to be good and not fight but that niggah! I was only out the hole for 10 days I don't know, Mom I got bigger working-out everyday Men thought I was a Little man before, now I'm the crazy man, 2 stabbing in two months of jail time, aint bad. But mom I will be good when I get out of the whole. It is just so hard not to fight. I LOVE U MOMMY
YOUR ONE AND ONLY SON
C.M.C

Then I reopen the letter from Booker T. and it read.
Dear Mrs. Booker T. Braddy the 4th

> *What's up, baby, I know this shit fucked up. However, what I want to share with you is that God is able and he is in control, so no matter what, you will always be my love, my wife for the rest of my life. I'm so sorry that I can't be there with you but know that my spirit and my prayers are with you always. Looking back over the years I know that I didn't always treat you the way I should and for that I'm truly sorry. You are the best thing that has ever happened to a bum like me. My prayer is that you can continue to hold on to our love as God continues to keep us strong. Because not even death can*

keep my love from you and we will be together again one day. Remember God gave us each other and he will put us back together again. I'm only gone for a while, got some thing I have to do to get straight so that we can receive the fullness of Gods grace. So don't worry God has not brought us this far to drop us, even if I go away for awhile I will be back again.

YOU ARE MY HEART AND MY SOUL, MY LOVE, MY EVERYTHING.

LOVE YOU SO MUCH.   LOVE

ALWAYS YOUR HUSBAND.

P.S SELL THAT DAMN LINCOLN, I'll GET A NEW ONE WHEN I COME HOME!

These two letters put the icing on the cake for me Mr. Journal' after thinking and thinking of how I will kill the marked man, I came up with two ways. One shot him in the head with a high power pellet gun. Pricing the skull, and entering the brain, two hits should do it. However, that way is too quick! I would like to see him suffer, like my-- boo, and my son is suffering right now. Dah, what about me, I'm suffering too shit. I think this bitch should join use. A pint size jar of gasoline just may do it, and then I can stand back a see his ass wiggle. Hell yes, it will be over this weekend, shit even if the fire department do come and put his ass out he will be done or should I say over done. Hi! Hi! Hi! The more I think about it the more I like it. I got this idea from a book called Gas Card, By Roxanne C Fredd.

In it there was a man stealing gasoline out of a car with a hose and a jar. The owner of the car saw the man, and started shoot at him. One of them hot

[235]

bullets hit the jar of gasoline setting dude on fire, in this book da hospital talked of how blessed dude was not to live with 4and 5-degree burns all over his body. The way that man died is the way I want the marked man to die. I got his ass this Sunday late night there will be less people. I will walk up on him at the strip joint. O-yes, I'mah cook-in me a niggah! B.B.Q. style

Marked Man Last Day!

The house phone was ringing so loud and 4 so long it had crossed over into my sleep. In my dream I keep reaching for the big white phone on the table but the table kept moving getting longer and I just can't reach it. It's ringing loudly and it kept on ringing. My sleep state eased away and reality told me

"Get up and get the phone."

Now some-what awake I grab the phone,

"Hello!"

"I love u, Baby, r- u -awake?"

"Yes my sweet husband I am awake"

"Tweet it is 11AM why are you still in bed, what time did you get to bed baby?"

"Clock read 6AM when I set the alarm and got into our bed baby."

"Ok, tell me Tweet why you did not get into bed until that time, and it

"Better be good bitch."

"BookerT It has been a long month of covert action but it will soon be over."

"What the fuck are you talkin about Tweet?"

Silence was on the phone for a sec; I'm thinking about that question, my stomach was flipping out of fear of the shit that would go down tonight. I had laid a plan but sometimes the best-laid plan can go wrong. One thing for sure the Fed phones are taped so we could not say too much.

"Baby there is a number of things about the marked man that's going down tonight and if all goes right I will have BBQ as a late night snack."

"Tweet the last time you where here visiting we talked about some shit and I told you that I will take care of it when I come home. So what part of leave shit be, did you not understand?"

"Don't get it wrong baby, I did understand you, but do you understand that this is something I got to do. You can say, because of the lick or the fuck over on you and my son, I don't care. He knew who I was when he set down to play the game, and he knew how I play my game, when I play! So now what — what—baby, now I just sit over on the side? Sit back and observe

That piece of shit everyday, walking around like he a winner" "Tweet, Baby
ok, look"

The phone beeped letting us know the call was at the end or near done.

*"Damn! I'll call you back later Tweet, please don't play your hand until I talk
to you again Ok?"*

Beep the phone went dead. As I hung up the phone, my thought was,

"I just wouldn't answer any more phones today.

Still in bed, I was hit with what ifs, so I can't sleep. What if things
don't go the way I planed it. My mind ran wild with all types of whit ifs for a
sec. I had to stop that line of thought because I do believe one can speak
things into manifestation. My mind then opened to the fact that I'm going
against An order from my husband; and it doesn't feel good at all. Shit, he
would be upset with me, but I had to do this one. Just like the nigga I killed in
Pittsburg; I just had to do it. This nigga had a shot-out with my mommy at an
after hour joint. She took one or two hits before she went down on the floor.
While she lie there gun out of bullets, he walked upon her and shoot her two
more times. Thank God! She did not die then, but it did leave her fucked up
with half a lung. That sick ass passion I had for killing back then has re-
awakened inside me today. My husband just—gone--half to understand, I
have got to get that marked man.

My head so full of stuff I just could not sleep, so I got up and got me some coffee. May as well take it out on the porch, to see what I can see down the street. Sure enough, it was on at the marked man's house. Just look at how he's getting all that money, good, he gone need it to buy a nice little box. I continued to enjoy my coffee, as my head started to work in over-time. It was as if my hatefulness sat on one shoulder and recovery sat on the other. Two voices took a turn to talk into my ears on my plan to kill the marked man.

Hate co-signing the plan of killing him. Recovery forcing me to look at all I have learned about the solutions in life journey. The solutions to having a good life go with making spiritual selections. Not to say be a goody –goody because no one is perfect, but I do have chooses. Make the right chooses and have a good day. Wrong choose I get a fucked up day. That was where the spiritual thing entered in play. If it don't feel right then it's not right in most cases. One voice told me,

"One-day he will get his, and I'm not God or his son so how dare I think of taking his life?" The other voice said"

"OK, all of that is true, but just for today, I am Jr. Jesus and I got this dude to night"...

Last Journal

Mr. Journal tonight was a night of reckoning and retribution it went just as sweet as I thought it would... On the lot of the tit club LiL Don sat inside of his car as he had for so many other nights doing what ever it was he does down in his lap. I strolled up slow and quite with the open can of fluid in my hand down at my side. Damn, his window is up think, think bitch. "Fuck—it, knock on the window"

Was what I whispered to myself, but first let's see just what this niggah is doing. O-shit, he was playin with his dick! The man was jacking off before going into the tit spot. He was so into it he didn't even see me standing there, the nasty fucker!

Mr. Journal when I taped on the window, I wish you could have seen that niggah jump out of shock of someone stepping up on him. He started shoving his dick down inside while redoing his jeans. Just a wonder he didn't zip his shit up in it. While he let down his window, I stood there shaking my head showing judgment on him.

"Damn I never even saw you standing there Tweet!"

Came forth out of his mouth then he twisted his arm to look at the time.

"What can I do for you, and what are you doing out here this time of the night?"

"I needed a light for my cigarette, I seen your car setting here as I came down the street so I stopped."

"O—Ok here" he reached down took up some matches from the middle

[241]

compartment of the car and handed them to *me not thinking I don't smoke no-*
-more dump ass. When that fact hit him, he looked up to say,

"Ah, you stopped smoking"

Those words cut short by the spraying of BBQ fluid all up into his face, chest
and legs. The shock of that shit hit him hard leaving him mentally stuck long
enough for me to strike the matches and toss them in on his ass. I walked
back-word enjoying that niggah jump-in and shoutin from the pain of the fire.
When the fire truck pulled up on the lot to put out the fire, there had not been
a sound coming from LiL Don's ass for about seven minutes. I felt very good
driving home. I even got a big ass smile when I drove pass his crib going to
park in front of my own crib.

Now out of the car and standing inside my yard I said,

"What Mr. Journal, what did you say? There goin to get me if I was dumb
enough to leave the can of BBQ fluid with my fingerprints on it. Ha, ha, you
got jokes Mr. Journal. No way can that happen because I got it right here, see
I got one more kill to do Mr. Journal and that would be you. Like I told you
before Mr. Journal the place where I come from I learned if two muthafucka
know your shit it aint no secret."

With those words I sprayed and lit the fire on Mr. Journal now, I got two
secrets.

Too bad no one knew when LiL Don rolled over in bed with the Feds it had to
be on one of his trips up state. He chooses to dish up his friends for his own
freedom. It is only through the revealing events that we know this to be true.

[242]

The Morning after Tweets Cookout

My good feeling I had about the death of the marked man was slowly trickling away. Seated on my front porch I sipped on my coffee as glimpses of last night danced in my head. The streets had a stillness I had not felt for a long time. This may have been due to the lack of drug sales at LiL Don's crib today or maybe not. My cup had gone up to my mouth to take another sip of coffee when the door to LiL Don's crib busts open.

"Boom!"

Out stumbled his wife waling loud as hell! Shit, she must have got the word on her hubby my marked man. I gazed at her entranced in pain that connected with lose of a love one. That shit started to touch my spirit. Fuck! I never thought about how his wife and other family members will feel after he was dead. He may have been a marked man to me, but someone did love him. Fuck-no, I have caused harm to those that had nothing to do with what was going down between us. Damn! I will get my Boo, back someday; however, her shit was gone forever! Now my spirit is not so up beat. I know what that feeling feels like from my losing my mom. That same pain I felt when the guards took my husband through the door without me. A powerlessness or call it an inability to do something to change what is happening at that time, at that place. Man, emotionally I began to brake as I re-felt that pain of absents of my husband that first night I went to bed. A blue Century full of crying people pulled up and parked. I can't see well due to the water inside of my own eyes. I had begun to cry not for the Marked Man but through empathy for the pain, his people are feeling. I wiped my eyes to see who I think is his sister Dee, and her husband along with four others. LiL Don's wife got even louder dropping down to her knees. Two more cars arrived while the sister Dee was helping the wife up off the concrete porch and into the house.

O-yes, there gona be a-lot-of people coming and going and it won't be about the sell of drugs this week. I feel rather bad about the entire thing but it was bound to happen someday. Shit we all come here to go one day! I figured that out when my mother died and when my husbands father died while he was in jail. That forethought don't stop the pain of lose, but it helps with the question of Why?

In Lil Dons case, I just had to help him along his way. A dog as nigga like that dude, aint no telling when he was gona be burned. Many cats wanted to kill LiL Don but they had kool aid for blood pumping to their heart. I don't know what that makes me for having the heart to kill a sucker that mess with mine. If it makes me hard, then I must be hard, if it says I'm sick or psycho then I must be, but I know one thing for sure,

"YOU WILL NOT FUCK WITH MINE AND LIVE TO LAUGH ABOUT IT!"

THE END

My only son Turtle

Raymond Jones Jr. GJ9570 Cresson, PA now holds a High school Diploma, not a GED along with certificates for Smart Money class and now attends Collage while in prison. He will be maxed out {4-1-2009}

My name is Booker T. and I know you all can feel me when I say,
"Stopping the use of drugs was the smartest thing I could have ever done for
myself. Attending school in fed prison to have my GED also was smart of me.
I now hold all the Certification, AC@R, 608, 609,410 Certification,
Environmental Protection Certified and HVAC ELECTRICAL! My dumbest
thing was thinking I could fuck with dope and guns and suffer no
consequences! Look at me! Here I am at FCI Gilmer reduced to a number
now"66945-061" I will come home capable of earning 60 dollars or more per
hour whenever I get to come home."

No-More Pimping

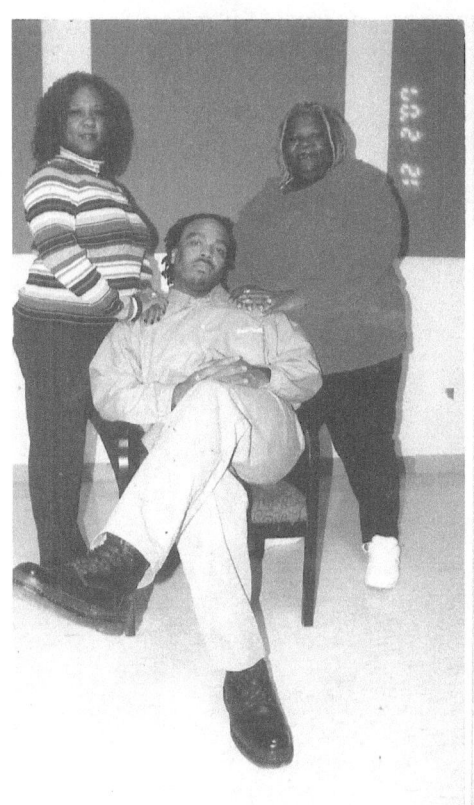 

Now To LiL Don,

If you should read these from the grave Marked Man, hear us when we say, *"this shit here, it's not personal it's all business. The code of (If it doesn't make dollars it don't make sense) applies here so, **Fuck—u-nigga.**"*

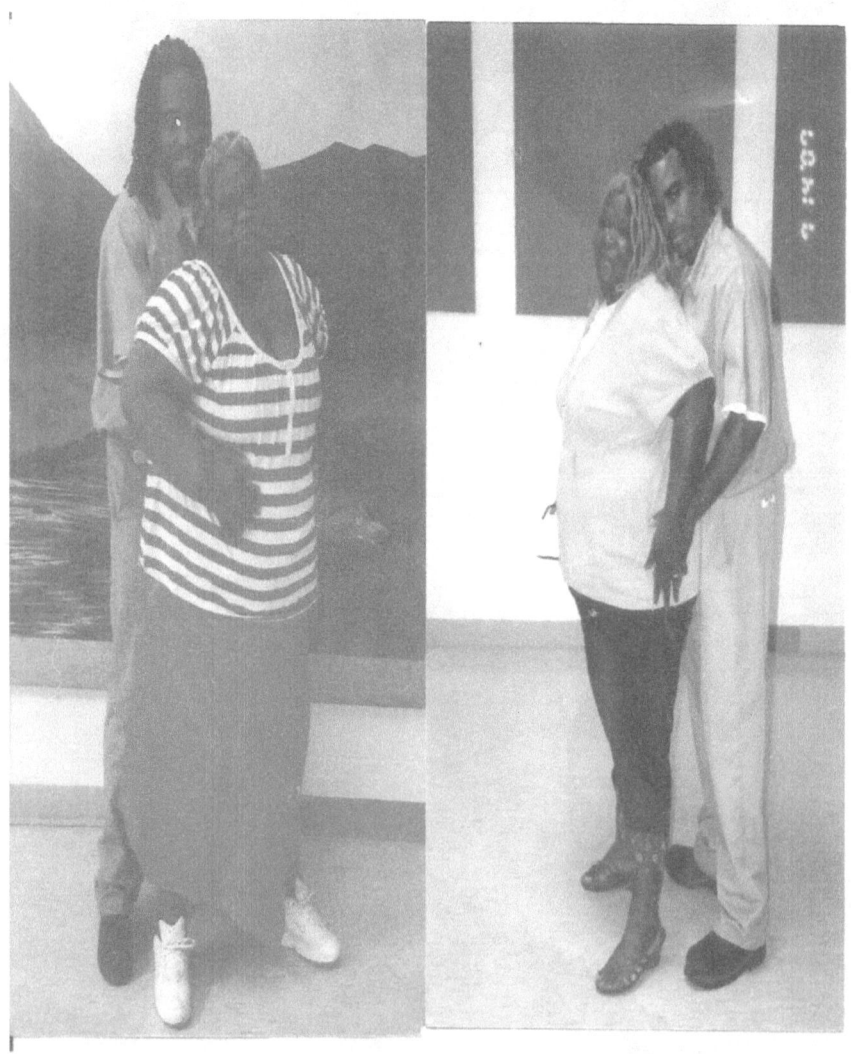

[249]